AF432698

BOURBON PENN

33

August 2024

Bourbon Penn Issue 33

August 2024

www.bourbonpenn.com

Myrtle Beach, SC

Editor:

Erik Secker

Copy Editing:

J. Scott Wilson

Cover Art:

Today and Tomorrow

copyright © by Jing Zhiyong

Very special thanks to:

Harley Carnell, Morgan Delaney
Milo K. Szyszka, Madeline Tredway

CONTENTS

FAT KIDS

— ■ —

Alex Jennings

Sometimes when I sleep, I wander too far from my body— or at least that's how it feels. It's like swimming out to sea, being caught by an undertow and knowing you've gone too far to make your way back to shore. Except I always do. It got worse during the Pandemic. My girlfriend taught in-person classes at Lusher, but I'd worked exclusively at home for years. Never having to be anywhere in the morning meant going back to bed as soon as I was done walking the dog and waking up at just any old time unless somebody needed something.

The first call I got that morning was my agent telling me that the manuscript for my first novel had been accepted for publication. I sat in my scratched-up red leather wingback in my bedroom office feeling full-body chills. So this was real now. I'd worked toward this moment for the last ten years—more—and here it was. I sighed.

"Thanks, Shawna," I said. "That's—that's a lot."

"How do you feel?" she said.

Still groggy and disconnected, I thought. "Good. I feel—"

I bit off the words as I saw another call incoming, this time, from my girlfriend Saadiqah. She had bad news about the hurricane in the Gulf.

"What's it doing?" I asked. The conversation was far from unusual. This happened most every year. A storm would enter the Gulf of Mexico, gather strength, and we'd play chicken with it, hoping it would veer away from New Orleans before we had to evacuate. You could say this mostly annual calculation was like the Sword of Damocles, but it wasn't that dramatic. It's just the sort of thing one got used to living here.

Diqah's voice dropped. "They say it's a four now."

"No shit?" I said. "Cat 4?"

My own personal rule had always been that we'd bug out for anything above a Category 2, but Diqah's beat-up Corolla wouldn't get us far, and rental cars were in short supply.

"What should we do?"

I shrugged. "Hit up Walmart like a couple of fat kids and get a good room up the street."

Many of the hotels in the Central Business District had generators, and even if the power went out in our apartment, it would likely stay on at the Loew's. So we raided the Tchoupitoulas Walmart for hurricane snacks, bundled up our dog Karate Valentino, and called a car.

The only hurricane I'd stuck around for was Isaac in 2012. Just me, my girlfriend at the time, and her cat. The only thing that truly frightened me was the sound of transformers cooking off as the driving rain clawed its way past their protective shells. They'd explode with these hollow pops that sounded like distant bombs falling—even over the freight-train roar of the wind and downpour. That storm was weak—Category 1, but it was slow, too. It squatted over New Orleans for a full 24 hours.

Isaac knocked our power out for four days. We spent a lot of time hanging out at the law office where Stell worked, streaming TV and eating sandwiches from Cochon Butcher, and on the fourth day, we arrived home to find our porch light burning again. For Ida, Diqah and

I got a room on the 20th floor. I'd never been up so high to observe a storm. Our view was of the rest of the CBD— Harrah's Hotel and Casino, the Hilton, the World Trade Center, and the brown band of the Mississippi reclining in its bed.

The hurricane came ashore like Count Dracula, in the form of a fog. I reasoned that the rain must be falling so hard that it seemed to foam up from the ground. As I stood watching out the enormous window, the hotel rocked back and forth like a cruise ship. We kept the news on, listening to the weather, and I was surprised to see that Karate wasn't worried. He took the thunder and lightning in stride. It was I who couldn't keep from staring in horror at the darkening river.

The hotel power went out around ten that night, with the storm still raging. By then, it felt like a giant had mistaken the building for a heavy bag and was practicing its best punches. Karate began to complain at the noise and the darkness and the terror that collected like ice water in my chest. I know I slept, but I'm not sure when or for how long. I dreamed that our room door opened softly the wrong way. Dark figures walked in, looked around. Someone stood at the foot of my bed. Someone else railed at and harangued me, but their volume had been turned down, and all I could hear was the most rudimentary shapes of their words—the sibilants, a plosive or two.

I woke the next morning to see the Mississippi flowing backward.

We hadn't bet that the entire city would go dark for weeks. We headed back to the apartment and languished in the heat, picking up donated meals from food trucks around town, swimming in the brackish courtyard pool to take the edge off. We didn't talk about it—not for some time, but once electricity was restored our home seemed smaller and grimier than ever. It was time for a change.

Of course, storm damage drastically affected the housing stock—that and the proliferation of short-term rentals in town. It was a good thing my own fortunes had already taken a turn for the better, or we would have been stuck in our shitbox for another year. As it was, we found a place and moved in November. That was around the time I got the first notification on Snapchat that Jon Reaux had joined.

Jon was one of the first people to welcome me into the scene when I started doing standup. Ten years younger than me, Jon had a star quality, a charisma to him, that I found undeniable. He was also lazy, unfocused, and seemed content to fuck around indefinitely. He could also be rude and dismissive, which I didn't take personally, but it stopped me short of considering him a friend.

I had no illusions about what comedy could do for me. I'd started too late to spend fifteen years in the trenches building my skills until I could tell jokes for a living. I was a writer, and comedy was something I did to blow off steam. I was decent at it—for a beginner—but I had no interest in the social push-and-pull of the comedy community. New Orleans was not the place to make it big in showbiz—it was somewhere to see and participate in excellent shows, and the instant gratification of getting laughs helped ease the pressure of the long waits involved in publishing.

One afternoon back in, oh, 2015, I was asked to perform on the Underwear Comedy Party. This was back when Joe Pettis was running the show, touring all over. I was morbidly obese, and gynecomastia had made my childhood a living hell, so before I got into standup I spent a lot of energy trying to deflect notice away from my size and shape. Comedy taught me to accept myself, that being the center of attention could be a good thing. Performing in my underwear didn't seem any scarier than getting onstage and talking into a mic in front of strangers, so I agreed.

On the night of the show, I arrived early. Jon was already there, still wearing his white and green work uniform. As my car dropped me off, he leaned against the wall that ran alongside Saint Claude Avenue, dragging on a Kool that looked so rumpled I was surprised it was intact enough to smoke. He was sweating, but it was barely more than eighty degrees out.

He was a good-looking guy. He was almost lanky, but without being tall or raw-boned. His complexion was maybe a shade lighter than my own. He'd worn his hair in an afro since we met—often uncombed. There was a hard, watchful playfulness to his expression.

I offered a handshake, but Jon turned abruptly away. I wavered for a beat, then shrugged, headed inside.

In those days, the Hiho Lounge was one of my favorite places to perform. It was small, but not so small as to lack a backstage. Smoking in bars and clubs had been outlawed by then, but there was a smoky quality to the light in there that made me feel almost like a real comic. The stage, raised a couple feet off the floor, even had a thrust to it.

I sat at a low table by the sound booth and pulled out my notebook to decide which jokes I'd go with tonight. I might stick with a setlist, and then again, I might not, instead riffing on how it felt to stand gigantic and nearly nude in front of the crowd.

A whiff of tobacco smoke told me that Jon had followed me inside. "We came up different."

I looked up to see him standing over me. "What?"

"We came up different, you and me. Our daddies stuck around."

It took me a moment to realize what he was talking about, and when I did, I squinted, irritated. "Sure," was the only response I could think of.

"Where your daddy from?"

I opened my mouth to respond and remembered the handshake he'd rejected. "Listen, man. I'm down to talk, but let me work my shit out first."

"Yeah," he said. "You good." He turned away.

I heard later that Jon was nervous about going up that night. Somebody told me he had insecurities about his own body. It hadn't surprised me to hear as much because many of the comics I thought would be perfectly at ease in their briefs were ready to jump out of their skin.

Still, I think about that exchange. I think about it a lot.

After a few years doing comedy, I started experiencing excruciating and unpredictable pain in my jaw which meant I had no idea when I'd have a pain-free five to fifteen minutes that would allow me to tell jokes to crowds. This was a problem I'd had off-and-on for years, but in 2017, the pain grew worse, more consistent.

I started doing comedy less and less. I'd get booked on shows or for readings and have to cancel at the last minute because I couldn't count on my jaw to cooperate at crunch time. It was time to finish the novel I'd labored over for years.

Jon attempted a move to New York and come back to New Orleans in a couple weeks when he ran out of money. That seemed like Jon all over, but don't get it twisted—I *knew* he would be a star. I knew that one day, I'd hear that Jon had been cast on *Saturday Night Live* or that he was getting a special on Comedy Central. All he would have to do was get out of his own way.

He spent some time back here licking his wounds, and then headed for LA. This time, the move seemed to take. He started performing out there, made friends. While I didn't follow him closely, it seemed he was doing well.

Then a mutual friend posted that he had died.

It was a waste, an impossibility. I spent hours hoping this was a tasteless bit—Jon trying to learn what the scene really thought of him—but he was truly gone.

Like a rock star, he'd died at 27.

• • •

It was a nightmare looking for a new apartment. Saadiqah and I toured cramped two-bedroom spots without central air, dishwashers, washer/dryers, and half the time, without so much as a fridge. Finally, Diqah and I decided that a large complex might be the way to go, so we toured a place at The American Can, an old factory/warehouse that had been converted into apartments years ago.

The complex is a landmark in itself, situated just across Moss Street from the final stretch of Bayou Saint John, a miles-long waterway that, at one time, had cut clear through New Orleans. The interiors still looked industrial, with painted-over metal sliding doors, concrete or scratched-up hardwood floors, and support columns occupying positions that must have been perfectly sensible when it was a factory, but now stood awkwardly here and there.

The apartment they showed us when we toured was bizarrely shaped, but it had two bathrooms, a dishwasher, washer and dryer. One of the reasons I'd been so slow to leave the old place was that it had an excellent saltwater courtyard pool. The American Can's pool was larger and lacked a deep end, but it would take the edge off during our boiling New Orleans summers. The only drawback to the place was that it was so close to the hospital.

Lindy Boggs Medical Center was once the best place in the region to handle transplants. It was a state-of-the-art facility up until Hurricane Katrina when it became a tomb for fifty patients. I lived in MidCity for about a year in 2009 before I moved Uptown, and I remembered walking by it then. I'd assumed someone would take it over and redevelop it, but nobody did. Instead, it was fenced in, neglected, and mercilessly tagged by street artists like Darpo, Cenac, and Fat Kids.

The first night I walked Karate past it, I had to turn my music all the way up in my headphones. No noise came from the hospital, but it was *loud*. I'm not talking about the screams and moans of the abandoned dead. It reminded me of being a kid, alone in the house, and hearing the air ring with silence. The lack of noise rippled through the vicinity like a sustained roar. I would have stopped walking by it entirely, but its position meant I'd have to stay off the Lafitte Greenway, which was one of the best neighborhood amenities we had—second only to the Bayou itself.

Besides: I didn't believe in ghosts.

· · ·

I've always been more active and capable than my size would suggest. My obesity has rarely kept me from going on walks, swimming, whatever activity I feel like taking. Diqah and I got Karate during the Pandemic because we're both heavy and we wanted a reason to take daily walks. He was a perfect physical motivator.

We took Karate on longer walks a few times a week. We'd traipse the entire length of the Greenway and back, or head over to City Park to march through the greenery or around Big Lake. This time, we'd walked up to the French Quarter, and the day exhaled boiling crawfish and cut grass. Sometimes, even at a distance, I could feel the hospital drawing nearer, as if in a dream where I stood rooted in place and the complex dragged itself to meet me.

As we walked, my mind slid from idea to idea, working out story problems, weighing this or that career move. As we neared the blacktop where the Farmer's Market erected itself every Thursday, the hospital felt like a thumb pressed against an Etch A Sketch. It didn't impede my thinking, but it was a distortion against the surface of my mind.

When we reached Moss Street, Karate insisted on investigating the giant flower sculpture situated near the street. Even with the hospital so near, I felt calm. I let my eyes drift shut and breathed a deep draft of the green city air.

The next thing I knew, Saadiqah glared at me, wide-eyed, as we stood on the greenway on the other side of Moss Street. "Hey, what?" I said. "What's wrong?"

"That's what *I* said!"

"Sorry," I said. "I checked out for a second, thinking about work." I realized then that she was holding Karate's retractable leash and that he was straining at its end, trying to resume walking toward some scent that had caught his attention. The hospital was louder than ever, with the volume and insistence of held breath.

I thought of that scene in *The Dark Knight Returns* when Bruce Wayne is startled awake by Alfred in the Batcave and finds that he's been sleepwalking again. I thought of myself standing here in my lounge pants in the middle of the night, staring blankly into the Hospital's vacant windows, and a cold prickle danced up the back of my neck.

"Sorry," I said again.

Just before we moved on, I noticed a new Fat Kids tag spreading above the largest windows near the roof of the main building. The tag was angular and ugly—the stylized letters seemed bent out of shape, but the stylization made the words mean something other than what they said.

• • •

Ever since my book came out—before that, even—I'd had a hard time getting rest. It didn't matter how late I slept or how deeply, I'd wake up feeling tired and washed-out. The situation didn't seem like cause for alarm. The Pandemic had worn on for years during which the fear of infection or of infecting others had only lifted for a few weeks at a time. Everyone I knew was worn out in one way or another. I tended to draw strength from spending time with my family back in the DMV, and I still felt the strain of missing and fearing for them for so long.

Saadiqah had been in New York for a few days when my gut started bubbling something fierce. I sat on the toilet, holding my belly and hoping whatever this was would respond to a little Pepto Bismol and some rest.

When I stood up and saw the toilet, I began to think otherwise. I tended to bleed now and then, never terribly much, but sometimes enough to excite my inner hypochondriac. There didn't seem to be any blood this time, but there was a black, tarry substance I'd never seen before, and as I stared at it, I felt dizzy.

It wasn't just that one trip, either. It was a string of them over the course of a day and a half. I began to feel even more tired, more out-of-sorts than usual. My memory, my consciousness began to waver, but how bad could the situation be if there was still no blood in the bowl? It took me a long time, *too* long, to haul myself half-naked into the bedroom. I stretched out diagonally across the king-sized mattress and felt the ocean of my consciousness lapping gently against the vault of my skull. I thought of Jon, dead for years. I thought of the quiet sands of the Sahara, and the pocked, mute surface of the moon. My thoughts circled tighter and tighter, then elongated as they drew down and away.

I hoped, as I passed out, that I would wake again.

I don't remember calling an Uber. I don't remember getting dressed or locking the apartment behind me. The next thing I knew, I was half-sitting, half-leaning to my left in the backseat of a Honda, staring at Saadiqah's photo as I waited for her to pick up.

"Hi, you!" she said. "How are you?"

"I think I'm pretty sick," I said. "On my way to the hospital."

"Which one?" she said calmly.

A glance out the window told me we were headed down Claiborne toward Harahan. "Oschner, I think. The big one."

"I'm coming."

"It's probably nothing," I said.

"Is it nothing?"

I felt heavy, and everything was slow.

"No."

Saadiqah and I met at a cookout out back of a murder apartment at the edge of the French Quarter. The killing was big news in the wake of Katrina when I moved to town. A guy had murdered his girlfriend with whom he had ridden out the storm and its aftermath. He hacked her up in the bathtub, then stashed her head in the oven and painted the bathroom and kitchen black. When he was finished, he got a hotel room up the street and spent every dime he had on pussy and narcotics before confessing everything in a note and jumping from a ninth-floor window.

A comedian friend of ours moved into the place years later, and when he invited me to a courtyard barbecue, I had to go. Saadiqah felt the same.

I'd only lived in New Orleans a few years, and I didn't believe in ghosts, so I wasn't surprised to find that the place bore no stain from the murder. It had been renovated, repainted, and outfitted with the latest appliances and décor. Vince was one of those comedians who moonlighted as a lawyer, so he had the place looking nice.

I recognized Diqah from a video I'd seen on Instagram where she danced her ass off with pompoms. She was tall and broad with sweet, heavy curves, dark dark skin, and bright, luminous anime eyes. Her complexion reminds me of my favorite soul song, "I'll Run Your Hurt Away" by Ruby Johnson. Like the vocals, Saadiqah's skin is rich and sonorous, and every time I touch it, I feel like I'm drawing a horsehair bow across cello strings.

She wore a fresh fruity scent I couldn't identify, but it was May, and it mixed with the faintly metallic edge of her sweat to make my head swim. All evening I found myself watching her closely, losing track of what she was saying as I tracked her movements and the motion of her lips.

We learned in conversation that we lived mere blocks from each other Uptown, so at the end of the night, we shared a cab. She sat quietly in the backseat, her fist balled loosely on her dark and ample thigh.

I said, "Saadiqah Ogunde, I think you're finer than a year's worth of speeding tickets."

She tried not to laugh but lost the battle. "Do you, now?"

"I surely do."

"… Then prove it …"

Our first kiss deepened quickly, and afterward I told our driver we'd only need the one stop. Diqah didn't get home much after that. About a year later, she moved into my apartment because I owned the nicer bed.

By the time Diqah joined me, I'd been admitted to the hospital, and I was on my second blood transfusion. The doctors felt reasonably sure that I had at least one ulcer and had done for some time. The black, tarry substance coming out of me was old and digested blood—and my hemoglobin was comically low. Our nurse Ms. Genevia was surprised I could speak or open my eyes.

I don't like to think how all this would have gone without Saadiqah. Or about the fact that sometimes there were three of us in that room.

Jon's death was heavy on the comedy scene. He wasn't the only one who'd left us over the years, but his absence was the most keenly felt—at least for me, and the comedians close to him.

I'd been told so often throughout my life that my size endangered my health. I'd tried diet after diet, and even when I worked out, all it got me was strong. That should have mattered to me more than anything, but what was all that effort worth if every tenth person I encountered still treated me like a circus freak?

That spring, everyone was talking about Ozempic, Wegovy, the new semaglutides that were helping people lose weight after lifetimes of trying. I'd seen crazes come and go. I remembered fad diets, new workout systems, and nutrition plans. I was more comfortable with my body, with myself, than I'd ever been, but winding up in the hospital spurred me to act. I asked my doctor for a prescription and started taking it—since I was diabetic, I didn't even have to pay.

For weeks, nothing happened. I honestly don't know what changed. Maybe it was that I recovered enough to boost my activity level without realizing it, but the weight started falling away like it almost never had.

Almost.

When I was twelve, my family moved to Paramaribo, Surinam because my dad was posted at the American Embassy there. With the boost in income, my family could hire me a personal trainer, and Mr. Leslie put me on a diet consisting mostly of bread and cheese with a normal meal every evening. I was also on my school's football team—I wasn't half bad, for an American.

I lost all the weight. All of it. People started treating me differently. Girls responded to me. I've never told anyone, but it broke my heart. When we moved to Tunis two years later, I gained back much of the weight. I didn't do it on purpose, exactly, but it wasn't an accident, either.

Diqah was younger than me by a few years. She was born in London to Nigerian parents and moved to Texas when she was twelve. That was the clincher for us, early on. She understood the trauma and excitement of moving to a strange country at a vulnerable age. Like me, her classmates had found her terminally weird, and she had faced the awkwardness of her teen years without the comforts of a home. She understood what it meant to be a fat kid.

I was seeing someone else at the time, had been for years. That relationship wasn't giving me what I needed, but I cared deeply for my partner and understood that neither of us was perfect. When we started dating, I explained to Diqah that I was polyamorous and that, for me, it wasn't so much a practice as it was an orientation. I felt I should be worried when Saadiqah said she was the opposite, but we had such fun together that my desire overrode what I thought of, at the time, as good sense.

I see how the world treats Black women. Dark-skinned ones, especially, and I hate it. I can't help but link it with the way I've been treated with my round bulk and manly tits. The fact that Saadiqah had ever been made to feel unattractive was absurd.

Our first kiss felt like celebrity. Like flashbulbs and red carpets. I felt like my best self, like the man I aspired to be. I felt transmuted, made beautiful by a sorcery of need. Denis Leary used to say that smoking builds character because, "Everyone deserves to know what it's like to want something more than anything else in the world and to get it over and over again." I never liked that joke, but I respected it, understood it. Saadiqah completed that understanding.

That's partly why, when she told me that she needed monogamy, I agreed to her terms. I simply could not let her go. The difference in our understanding of relationships and desire worries me from time to time, but I've never regretted my decision.

Not once.

• • •

Sleep got rocky when the weight started melting off, and all the while I kept getting those goddamn Snapchat notifications from "Jon." I never figured out the app. I got it because most of my comedian friends were on it, but I knew as soon as I downloaded and took a look at it that I didn't care to understand.

My doctor watched me closely, testing my blood every couple weeks, but all my numbers did was improve. Blood pressure dropped, evened out, A1c plummeted below the diabetic range, and by October, I'd lost roughly 90 pounds. I had a lot of clothes that stopped fitting during the Pandemic, and every so often, I would try to and fail to get into a shirt I hadn't worn in years. One afternoon, Diqah and I attended a cookout at the Peristyle in City Park, and all of a sudden, a pair of slacks I hadn't gotten into since 2019 swam on me—large enough that I knew I couldn't dance without a belt or suspenders.

My body felt stronger—*younger*, even. But there was a shadow at the edge of my consciousness: Before she left me, Stell had said, "There's a reason you haven't lost weight since we've been together. Something in you likes you this way. It wants you to stay sick."

It had crushed me.

I was proud of my achievement, shedding so many pounds, even with the help of a wonder drug, but I was conflicted. When I looked at myself nude in the broad bathroom mirror, saw myself shrinking, a small voice whispered at the edge of my mind: *What are you doing? If you're not big, what are you? Why would you want to be small?*

There's a dream I've had since I moved to New Orleans: I take a wrong turn walking to work. It doesn't matter where I'm working at the time. The dream is situated in an eternal present where I leave home every day. I take a wrong turn somewhere in Black Pearl or Gentilly, or in the Bywater, and the street signs stop making sense.

I keep walking as the hour creeps later and later. I check my phone to find I can't read the time. The readout shows digital runes like the wrist display in the Predator movies. No matter what I see there, it spurs me to turn more often, losing myself more and more. After a while, it's evening, and I still haven't made it to the office/café/school, and I know I'm going to be fired. Eventually, I come to a motel, the same one my brother and I stayed in the first time we visited New Orleans in 2003.

Nobody's at the front desk, so I look around the property for someone who can give me directions. Eventually I come to a room with an open door, and inside are three cops with deep shadows distorting their faces— almost like bank robbers wearing pantyhose masks. The policemen are busy subduing a lanky, light-skinned Black man with an afro shorter than Jon's was last time I saw him. He's wearing a gray tweed blazer with elbow patches even though the air smells of rust, orange oil, and baking heat.

One of the cops kneels with his knee pinned against the man's back. The others are speaking gibberish, brandishing their batons. Sometimes they hit the man, and he cries out, his voice high and thin like an infant's. There is an awful familiarity to the vision. It frightens and saddens me, but it isn't a shock. I know the man being beaten is dead, has been for years, and that this is the Dead Side of New Orleans.

One cop looks up at me. He stabs the first two fingers of his right hand toward his eyes, then points them in my direction. *I'm watching you. I'm watching you. I'm watching.*

One day, I'll die, and I'll return to this room to take the man's place. Every time I have the dream, I wonder whether that day has already come, if this is my chance to relieve him.

It never is.

I started awake to find the air dancing invisibly. Diqah slept next to me, snoring lightly, lying on her side as if she'd fallen from a great height. I slid the fingers of my left hand into hers, which usually calmed me after a nightmare, but this time, nothing changed.

It took me a moment to realize it, but my phone had just chirped for my attention. It was set to Do Not Disturb, so no notifications should have come through. Moving slowly, as through water, I picked up the phone to read the screen. I expected it to tell me again that Jon had joined Snapchat, but instead, the notification read, *Jon Reaux has sent you a chat:*

u busy???

I stared at the message for a long time, fully aware what my response would be. Finally, I typed it in:

no wazzam?

His response took long enough for me to wonder whether one of our old mutuals was pulling a shitty prank.

fat kids

come 2 fat kids

sumn to show u

fat kids

fat kids

fat kids

fatkids

fat

fat

I sucked my teeth. People talked about closure. We talked about symmetry. Story brain and pattern seeking were baked into our collective psychology, but if life had taught me anything, it was that life was *not* Story. Life was messy. Humans applied structure to the stories we told ourselves so that we could live with our pasts, live with ourselves. The dead didn't communicate through phone apps. They didn't resolve out of the mists of uncertainty ...

Unless they did. I'd been wrong before ...

k. gimme a min.

When I stepped onto Toulouse Street, the hospital was quiet—which worried me more than if it had been at a full blare. I cut through the Wrong Iron's parking lot to the

Greenway and saw that the complex wasn't abandoned anymore. No graffiti. No broken windows. The lights inside were on and burning.

The sight hit me like a sucker punch. It was as if I saw into an alternate New Orleans where nobody had been left for dead or euthanized when the city drowned.

Years ago, after Stell left, I would go for walks around Central City because my apartment was too small and close for the self-loathing I felt. I'd take photos of blighted buildings and post them to social media with the caption, "ME IRL."

I pulled out my phone to aim it at the hospital, but on the screen, the place looked as it always had. Windows gaping empty, chain link fence bordering Conti, tags crowding every surface. I photographed it anyway, nine or ten times, posted each one without context or explanation. I didn't realize until I'd finished that if Diqah woke to find me gone and saw the posts, she'd be terrified.

I knew I should turn around, return to bed, keep inhabiting this world—but I didn't. I cut through the vacant lot the bar used for overflow parking and crossed Conti to the complex. No tags stood out on the hospital's outer walls, but I knew where to go.

· · ·

I saw a ghost once. I saw *something*, I mean.

Before I moved uptown, I lived on St. Peter and Dauphine. It was a lovely little place with black and white checkerboard linoleum in the kitchen, stainless steel appliances, and a few of those bricked-up fireplaces you see everywhere in New Orleans. Back then, my morning routine had me waking early, making myself a cup of tea, and spending an hour sipping thoughtfully and planning out my day before I had to leave for work.

One morning, just like any other, I had made my tea and turned around to head back to my room, but the sight of a strange white man standing in the dim of the living room stopped me in my tracks. He wore old-timey clothes—breeches and a waistcoat with riding boots—and his hair was tied back with a maroon ribbon. He seemed as shocked to see me as I was to see him.

I cried out. It wasn't a shout of terror, it was involuntary, like a fart or a sneeze. I jerked my tea-bearing hand in the air and spilled some on my wrist. It stung me at a remove—I registered the pain, but it didn't make my list of priorities.

The man and I regarded each other for a few more seconds, and then he wasn't there. He didn't disappear or fade, he just wasn't there anymore. Instead, there was the collection of shapes—the outline of my brother's L-shaped desk and executive chair, a bust of Mozart sitting on the mantlepiece ten or eleven feet in front of me, the ferret cage ...

From time to time, our blender would turn itself on, and we would joke that a ghost was trying to make itself a margarita. Neither of us got a haunted vibe from the apartment, and as transplants to the city, we'd brought with us a healthy dose of DMV skepticism.

I can't say for sure that what I saw was a ghost. The man I saw didn't look dead. His cheeks were ruddy. His hair—it seemed like real hair and not a wig—was carefully combed and tied. His clothes weren't meant for the grave. When I recall the incident, his expression clinches it for me all over again. He was truly astonished—as if I had appeared to *him*. He was probably appalled to see a Negro in pajamas and a dressing gown make himself a cup of tea like he owned the place.

This is what I mean when I say I don't believe: I don't know what I saw. I don't understand the circumstance. Sure, I could assume I'd seen the spirit of a man who had been dead for hundreds of years, but if that's possible, then it's also possible that he and I somehow saw each other across time. That both of us were perfectly at home in our eras, going about our daily lives, and the veil of years had thinned enough for us to see each other.

There was no message attached unless we ourselves were the message.

A few weeks ago, I watched four teenage boys pry a back door open and head inside the hospital. I never saw them come out, but if something had befallen them, it would have made the news, right? I try not to think about the fact that these were a bunch of Black kids. What if nobody had missed them, and they had disappeared like smooth stones dropped into a pond?

People who have ventured inside claim to have heard the screams and sobbing of stranded patients, seen spectral doctors scrambling in a losing battle to save their charges. A friend of a friend even claims to have been chased out of the complex by "a fuckin demon, my nigga!"

None of those stories sound right. In them, the teller knows exactly what's going on. They're adamant about their experience. *I know what I saw, baby!* It's the *certainty* in anecdotes of the supernatural that makes them so hard for me to believe.

Our bodies shape the way we experience the world. The way we propel ourselves across it, communicate with each other, with other creatures. How can it be so easy to converse with bodiless spirits? People tell stories of encountering ghosts, cryptids, angels—and their tales are strangely basic. People in the Bible collapsed with seizures when heavenly spirits appeared, and you're telling me that when one turned up at a red light and leaned into your passenger window to tell you to turn left instead of right at the second light down that you felt just fine?

Dark fell on me like a velvet curtain when I stepped into the hospital. It was like being waterboarded by unsight. I still felt a floor beneath the too-thin soles of my shoes, so I trusted my body to anchor me to myself, to something familiar. My footsteps made no sound.

Before we moved in together, Stell lived in a slave-quarter apartment in the Vieux Carre. Her place was on the second floor, past the courtyard, but to come and go, we had to use a narrow hallway to access the street. The overhead light in there was broken and the landlord had never fixed it. That corridor always seemed much longer and darker than it should have—almost like a metaphor.

That ice-water sensation filled my chest again. It buoyed my heart, radiated through me in waves, and every time I felt the darkness lap into my throat, I expected it to wake a raw red scream. Just when my unused voice began to feel like it would choke me, a breeze gusted my way carrying the aromas of coffee, steamed milk, and frying dough. All at once, I found myself in City Park, standing on the sloping bridge that ran between the sculpture garden and Café du Monde.

My surroundings resolved like the shifting of a dream—that moment when one place becomes another, when one life and history fade in favor of some revised circumstance. I don't know if other folks dream this way, but I've dreamed entire lifetimes which segued into other lives, complete with their own memories of fictional pasts. I shivered as I waited to understand where I was, what I was doing, and all I could think about was Jon's only TV appearance.

Just before I quit comedy, a documentary production had come to town. They were taking looks at comedy scenes around the country, and a comedian couple who actually owned a house had put on a show in their backyard, served pizza, packed the place out. Most anybody who wanted to had gone up. Jon had performed one of his best sets ever, where he complained about wearing a paper hat to serve coffee and beignets here in the park. As I crossed toward the café patio I was sure I'd see Jon wearing his uniform, his ridiculous hat canted jauntily on his fro.

He wasn't in the abbreviated parking lot by the coffee stand or on the patio with its crazed ochre-and-yellow floor. Only one seat was occupied, and the man sitting there was not the one I wanted to see.

Meeting yourself is not like looking in a mirror. It's not like watching yourself on a screen. To see your living breathing doppelgänger filling out a wrought-iron chair, his rolls bunched beneath his arms is— He must have had his hair cut just that day; he smelled of Barbicide and Afro Sheen. The slight sourness of breath told me he still smoked cigarettes from time to time. The sight of him was worse than disorienting. It was sickening. Especially when I realized that some small part of me had expected this.

When I was very ill from the blood loss, Saadiqah told me I looked pale. That pallor, that washed-out quality wasn't visible to me in a mirror—but it was now. So was the difference in weight. One look at this other self told me he weighed significantly more than I did.

I had frozen in mid-step. My body wanted to continue past the café, past the Peristyle, and on home as I had so many times on my walks with Karate—or just turn around and head the other way—but I couldn't. The paralysis only broke when I resumed my approach.

I sat across from him.

"It worked," he said evenly.

"That was you contacting me? Pretending to be Jon?"

He shook his head. "Jon helped. He's here somewhere."

"Working the café?"

He scowled. "Of course not," he said. "Would you?"

"No, but— I don't know how this works."

"Would it help if I told you it was all in your head?"

"Is it?"

His grin was a humorless display of crooked teeth. "Not at all."

I shut my eyes, took a steadying breath. I was terrifically angry. Baldwin said that to be a Black man in the United States and even a bit conscious was to be in a state of rage almost all the time. It was one of those truths that made me feel spied-on—one of the truths that made Baldwin difficult for me to read. This anger, this loathing, felt dirty and craven.

I opened my eyes. "What do you want? An apology?"

"If that's your way of asking whether you killed me, the answer is yes. You did. But it took more than you. More than a simple desire, or even your action. It was a million little things. I suffocated. I kicked, I screamed, and I begged. I told you stories."

I shook my head. "The stories are mine," I said. "Only I could tell how I survived. How I've kept everything from fucking caving in! How I—how I—connected with something beyond me. Only I could tell what it felt like for me to live divided from everyone and everything."

"I was there with you."

"Is that what this is? You want me to tell you I miss you?"

"It's not that you're killing me that bothers me," he said. "It's that you're so cruel about it. What did I do to deserve what you've made of me? Why do you want to lock me in that hospital? Why do you want me in that motel room getting killed over and over by those cops?"

It took effort to keep my shoulders from rising to my ears. "I won't do this with you," I said. "You know why."

"Say it."

I shut my eyes again, inhaled through my nose. The trickiest thing about rage is that it is often a mask for deep sorrow.

"Stell was right about me," I admitted. "I couldn't get rid of the weight because something bad was alive in me. Some small sniveling part of me that held me back. *You.*"

"You decided to kill me as soon as you could figure out how to do it without killing yourself."

"Yes," I said. "I hate you. Oh, *people are* mean. Oh, *the world is* hard! Oh, *people don't understaaaaand me.* Nigga, *fuck* you."

My words fell onto the table between us and just lay there for a moment as we regarded each other in silence.

This wasn't what I wanted. I had hoped for some impossible closure with Jon, or my memory of him, not a confrontation with my own self-pitying ghost. I'd been so proud, believing I'd transcended the worst of my limitations, but how true could that be when I looked on myself with such loathing and disgust?

"It wasn't my fault," he said. "What happened to us wasn't because of me. Our pain didn't come from me—not at first."

"So what?" I said. "You're the part of me I can get rid of. I could say I didn't know I was killing anybody. I could say I didn't mean to cause you pain."

"Lies," he said.

I nodded. "Yeah."

"Good luck getting out of here without me," he said. "You pretend nothing good in your life came from me. Like I never taught you to tell jokes or write poetry."

"Come on, Alex," I said gently. "You know good and well that I would give all that up in a heartbeat to be rid of you forever."

His face fell. More than anything, in that moment, I was amazed by his anguish and dismay. How could a piece of myself misunderstand me so thoroughly? The difference between us was not that I was better or more capable than he. The difference was that when I left here, to walk back into the dark of the hospital, I would *crawl* through that blackness if I had to, knowing that if I kept on, crossed the Greenway back to my apartment, I'd find Karate snoring in my red leather chair, yipping softly as he chased rabbits through his dreams. Diqah would be lying on her right side, her smooth left leg bent at the knee, her pillow clenched like an old-fashioned telephone receiver between her cheek and her shoulder.

I don't tell you this to prove myself a better man than that other self or to reveal that I am worse. I tell this story as faithfully, as truthfully, as I can, because it is the least I can do for the man I was.

He'll never rest in peace, and he deserved better.

■

Alex Jennings is a comedian, educator, and award-winning author whose writing has appeared in Current Affairs Magazine, pseudopod.org, *and* New Suns, *volumes 1 and 2. He is an instructor of Popular Fiction at the Stonecoast MFA program as well as a columnist for* The Magazine of Fantasy and Science Fiction. *His debut novel,* The Ballad of Perilous Graves *was released by Orbit/Redhook in 2022. His fiction and poetry have been short-listed for numerous awards including The Ernest J. Gaines Award, The Ray Bradbury Prize for Speculative Fiction, the Locus Award for Best Debut Novel, and the World Fantasy Award. He is the winner of the 2023 Compton Crook Prize from the Baltimore Science Fiction Society. He lives and works in Baton Rouge, Louisiana. As of this publication, he has lost 125 lbs and counting. Find out more at www.alexjennings.net*

THE LIGHT IN THE HEART: A HAUNTING

— ▪ —

Valya Dudycz Lupescu

Houses talk. Well, some of them do. Most of them did. Many don't anymore.

Like you.

Like any love story, your beginning is every golden shade of honeymoon: years of barefoot dancing and bed bouncing, freshly painted walls that echo happy moans and hungry cries, air filled with rye bread baking and coffee brewing, shiny oak floors for block building and board game playing, a paper chain of daily meals around a long barnwood table—the light in your heart a solstice sun.

Time flows through your halls and scatters sand as the parts that once worked begin to grate against each other, until overwound and mishandled they break down. Your family stops dancing together in the kitchen, no longer wish-watching for stars on the porch. Dust thickens around the crystal vases, and no one replaces the batteries in the wall clocks.

Shared stories sharpen into barbs until everyone feels attacked all the time. They stop taking off their shoes when they come inside. No one wipes the smudges off your mirrors. The television stays on, and everyone answers the phone on the first ring. You get divided into zones and the doors stay closed. You feel yourself breaking up into pieces of a puzzle that no one remembers they started.

Hands that potted plants and caressed fabrics onto your walls stuff scrapbooks and mismatched socks into cardboard containers. Afterthoughts of Halloween costumes and handmade ornaments shoved into black bags destined for a pile ... someplace else.

Not here. Not with you.

On the last day of boxes and tearful glaring, no one cares enough to wash your floors.

No one comes back.

At first the quiet is a balm: the squeak and settling of boards, squirrels on the roof, bees buzzing around woodpecker holes. Rains rolling down windowpanes and the howl of a displaced dog distract you from the relics: baggies of baby teeth left on the closet shelf, dusty icons forgotten in the dining room hutch, wedding dress molding in the basement—discarded promises.

Weeds stretch taller through cracked concrete as the mail pile stops growing. Cold, damp air enters with the opossum and rabbits, cats and bats. The wallpaper curls; the wood warps; the paint peels. You feel yourself fade with each missing shingle and cracking crown molding. Winter hurts the most, heart-punch of hollowed-out rooms where holiday nights were once filled with fairy lights and couch cuddling.

You grow weary under the weight of waiting.

Until a steel-toed boot crashes against your front door, and footsteps in your foyer echo down into the basement where you have settled into a dispirited haze. Nervous giggling as they carve cartoons into the banister and write their names in marker on the green deco tile of the kitchen. They hide things in your pantry and sleep on blankets in front of the fireplace they have filled with candles, wax rivers running onto your planks. They paint the walls with rainbows and hang wrinkled bed sheets in front of the windows. They leave garbage in the bathroom and take away your crystal doorknobs and glass sconces. Smoke damages your ceiling and they make a hole in the upstairs floorboards; but every time they touch you, you tell yourself it's love.

You wait for them, their loud music and cigarette kisses, comic books and combat boots, and for a while it feels like family. Then one-by-one they stop coming, until the last remains alone inside for weeks, the smell of sickness heavy on his breath as he kisses your door knocker on his way out. "Wish I lived here for real," he says.

You never see him again.

A few times a year, when the leaves have fallen and the night is crisp, gaggles of children come with hushed voices in search of ghosts and goblins. They practice fear, looking in your darkest nooks for secrets but finding only the cold.

You stop holding your breath every time a new hand touches your doorknob. With their rock throwing and pissing contests, you feel something harden. You ache for warmth, and anger creates its own kind of heat.

You dream of burning.

That is when the creatures crawl down your chimney, Old World monsters who value a well-built house without human blight. Mouths wide with pointy teeth grinning, they camouflage onto your walls so their skin matches yours—they reframe the way you see yourself.

They wait for the children, watch from the eaves when clowns and robots, witches and skeletons burst in. Weaving a web of whispers and reflections around them, the creatures feed off the fear you can see like smoke in the air. After the children run away screaming, the creatures swallow the thick, delicious dread with wide-open mouths. They lick fear off the floorboards and catch it dripping raw from the ceiling onto their long, pointy tongues. They dance joyfully through your halls, kiss your corners, and tell you what a wonderful house you are.

You learn to love your cracks, to lean into the cobwebs and jagged, broken bits. You exhale your groans onto the wind, shake your shutters, creak unapologetically into the wide eyes of uninvited guests. You find ways to hide your fearsome family when it's necessary, holes that appear, walls that vanish, the impossible stretching of shadows.

Yuletide comes, and in the way of old offerings, they bring you gifts: evergreen branches, a glittering bauble, a gingerbread man, a string of garland. They light a fire and gather together in front of the hearth with their treasures, caressing your floors and walls with claws and fur fingers, the sound of their singing and stomping and beating of wings—a carol carried by the wind under the sills and out of your weep holes.

A knock at the door and your family explodes into happy cackles and hungry howls, scattering into shades of midnight as the flames of your hearth grow brighter and more inviting.

You have learned that love always leads to being haunted, so you open..

■

Valya Dudycz Lupescu is the author of Mother Christmas, The Silence of Trees, Forking Good, *and* Geek Parenting. *She is also the editor of* Embroidered Worlds: Fantastic Fiction from Ukraine and the Diaspora, *published in 2023. Valya earned her MFA in Writing from the School of the Art Institute of Chicago. Her work has been published in* The Year's Best Dark Fantasy & Horror, Ukrainian American Poets Respond, Kenyon Review, Strange Horizons, Mythic Delirium, *and others. Valya has been making magic with words and food for 25 years, incorporating traditions from her Ukrainian heritage with practices that honor the Earth.*

BEYOND THE FLY CURTAIN

Françoise Harvey

The bell above the door rings when they go in, even though the shop is closed. And even though the shop is closed, the jangling racket conjures Missus Lambert from the mysterious cave beyond the faded fly curtain. She flicks the strands of beads from her curlers as she emerges, queenly. Because the shop is closed, she doesn't stop behind the counter like she normally does. She carries on down the aisle, comfortable slippers slapping the linoleum.

She looks smaller, cozier, than she does from her usual position of power, presiding over the till with a view of the whole shop. Scary, actually, how much she always seems to see, and how – despite the smile, despite the welcoming of customers – always there is a hard gimlet glint to her eye. Measuring you.

Now, the gimlet glint is veiled by reading glasses. She views her two visitors with less of a laser stare, forgoing the raking measure of how much their pockets are bulging, how their sleeves are sitting against their arms – maybe in part because they've worn T-shirts, despite the cool morning, to show they mean no harm. Still, paying mind to Missus Lambert is a generational memory, and so they nod close to bowing as she approaches. This is her kingdom, and just pushing the door open against the "closed" sign required a stiffening of the spine.

"Here for the job, Missus Lambert," says one. "Mam sent me."

"And me," pipes up the other, a bit quivery.

"Which job?" says Missus Lambert, taking off her glasses and squinting at them as though she's posted a whole corporation's worth of possibilities in the paper, not strung a single sign asking for a "deliverer of goods" on brown paper in the window.

"That one," says the quivery lad, pointing. Missus Lambert narrows her eyes at the tip of his finger, and he drops his hand fast. "Deliveries. Mam said we'd to be here 6 a.m. on the dot."

"Oh, yes," she says, after a pause just long enough to make them both squirm. "Both of you, then? Follow me."

She turns and stamps back up the shop. Back straight, slippers somehow now tough as boots, as though they'd caught her unawares before, though wrong-footing Missus Lambert is unimaginable. She clatters back through the fly curtain, into the dark space beyond. They follow her, hesitantly, urging each other to go first with nods and slowed shufflings of the feet.

"I'll need you to move quicker than that!" calls Missus Lambert from beyond the curtain, and they take a collective breath and part the beaded strands.

No one can remember a time when the shop wasn't there, though there surely was one. It couldn't have existed before there was a house, a settlement, a village, a town, surely? There's a small brass plaque over the smartly painted doorframe that says "Proprietor Elsie Lambert: purveyor of goods and alcohol by permission of ----- Est. -----" The year and the name can read whatever you like, depending on the slant of the shadows and the glance of the light, and some people would say that the year is older than the date on the first stone in the cemetery – also scuffed and weathered to unreadable. Might say Lambert. Might not. It's all in keeping with the magic of the place.

If magic's what you'd call it. There's no magic in the look of the building. It might have stood alone at one point, but now it's the lit-up end of a row of close terrace houses – there's a jagged line in the bricks where the red changes from old to older to drywall. The display window frames are painted bright green, the walls are white, the painted stones smoothed by time. There's nowhere to park outside the shop, but people will make the effort to walk to it, with good reason: Elsie Lambert can conjure just about anything that's asked for, given a few minutes to rummage in the dark, secretive space beyond the fly curtain, which hasn't been changed in years.

There's rumors of a smugglers' tunnel, or a magic box, or a carpet bag a la Mary Poppins back there, depending on your age. Nothing seems too outlandish, because here's a fact: Even in lean times, the shop has what's needed for the people that frequent it, and it always has done – even when it was Elsie's mam, or grandma, or great-grandma running the place. There's a strong likeness between them all, according to the old people. In looks and ability and attitude. All the Lamberts could read a face for true want and get what was needed for a price the buyer could afford, though no one ever shared what was paid, if a deal was done.

"There's families in this town wouldn't exist if it weren't for the bitshop. They'd've starved to the end of the line," said Mam, once. She said it to the boys harshly, along with a string of other reminders about respect, earning it, paying it, making amends. They'd been caught red-handed trying to roll a packet of Polos from the shelf up into their overlong sleeves. The police weren't called, and they weren't even banned. The look in Missus Lambert's eye when she'd said "Hoi, now, and what's that up your sleeve, lads?" ever so quietly, and the way every other person in the shop had turned suddenly, like soldiers under Missus Lambert's command – it had near scared them to pissing themselves right there in front of everyone.

"Some folks need to do it to learn not to," Missus Lambert had said graciously to their Mam. "We'll talk later."

And Mam had gone very red and swallowed hard, herded them out and smacked their ears in the street. They'd only ever gone back in with lowered eyes since – because they'd had to go back, of course. It was unthinkable to go anywhere else.

Beyond the fly curtain is a perfectly ordinary room, walls painted blue, and bare apart from a calendar set to the wrong month and the wrong year. Two more doors – one open, stairs behind it, carpeted. Missus Lambert must sleep above the shop. The other is set into the far wall and can only lead farther back into the terrace of houses. There's an armchair, worn, and two sturdy wooden chairs. They know those chairs – they're the very ones brought out those years ago, for them to sit and await their punishment, the seats polished by years of shifting, guilty bums. There's a tidy desk in one corner, with a small, ancient telly. It's got a coat-hanger aerial on top and the screen's showing the inside of the bitshop in HD. Delayed, the video seems to be, for whatever good that is: they just catch sight of their own backs passing through the curtain. Missus Lambert settles herself in the armchair, nods them toward the wooden chairs. She steeples her wrinkled fingers under her chin and considers them.

"Polos," she says, eventually. "That was you two, wasn't it?"

They blanch. One nods, chewing his lip; the other points at his twin, scowling. It's infuriating, still, after all these years, to be scooped up in his twin's misdeeds. Missus Lambert cackles. "No honor among thieves, eh. Good to know. I suppose you know what the job, is then? Your mam said?"

"Newspapers ...?" says the one that pointed, trying for enthusiasm. He trails off. Shivers – it's colder in this room than in the shop: no windows, no warmth. Missus Lambert raises her eyebrows.

"Newspapers?" she says. "Where do you see people with newspapers anymore? No, I move with the times, and the newspapers, what few sell, that's in hand."

The one who tried to steal the Polos catches on faster. "It's everything else, isn't it. 'Cause the internet ..."

"Exactly," Missus Lambert leans back in her seat. "I've seen off supermarkets, farmers markets, hypermarkets. Always given a personal touch and been able to get my hands on the products people want. But I'm not blind to change ..." This was true. The bitshop had a DVD of every film produced, it seemed, ready to rent and sell from the moment someone in town bought its first DVD player. They've since vanished, of course. "And this is something people need – things delivered, the next day they say. The *same* day, even, without them setting foot from their house. And so that's what we'll be offering. We – that includes you. I'll be minding the shop, you'll be taking the goods out."

"What kinds of goods?" asks the not-thief. "Like? ..." He thinks of all the stories, of the things Missus Lambert has supposedly provided from the back of this shop.

"Food. Paper. That sort of thing," she considers him. "Anything more complicated, they'll need to come here. At least to begin with. We'll see how it goes. Test run. Remember that – this is a test run. The first sign of trouble ..." she cocks her head and to the one that pointed, that's more threatening than anything she could say out loud.

"We haven't said we want the job yet," says the thief. He's folded his arms, straightened his back. Acting like he's forgotten everything they were told, and maybe he has. His brother shoots him a pleading look.

"Would you still be sat here if you didn't? Would your Mam let you keep your room if you don't go back and say we're straight and you've gainful employment?" Missus Lambert is tapping one finger, very lightly, on the flowery fabric of the armchair. Behind her there is a faint squeal of hinges, and the door in the far wall, not properly shut, moves in a non-breeze. *Tap tap tap.* The lad's boldness is gently squashed by her fingertip.

"We could get jobs at the warehouse," stammers the one who pointed. "Loads of jobs going there." The other stares at the door, still swinging slowly open.

"Delivery," says Missus Lambert. "Sure. But delivery with no soul to it and no heart to it. Here's a job you can be proud of. And I pay well. And I'll teach you all the secrets of this place, maybe. If it's a fit. Or not." The door swings squealing open all the way, hits the wall behind with a crack. Missus Lambert doesn't even blink.

They say yes without checking the wage.

· · ·

There'd been a game for a bit, when they were even younger, when they still dared cheek Missus Lambert a bit. Not just them, of course: the whole rowdy lot of their class in school. On Fridays, it was, they'd dare each other things to ask for. Impossible things. You'd get your pocket money Saturday morning and spend Saturday afternoon seeing if you could catch Missus Lambert out with your requests.

They never could, mind. She had the measure of them – they couldn't have been the first to try it. They'd asked – for elephants; camels; a rocket ship; nail polish that turned from green to blue. And every time she'd twinkle at them, and accept their 25p in return for a little plastic figure of whatever they asked for, or in the case of the nail polish, exactly that. But she knew – she knew when the longing was real. You didn't really want a massive rocket ship in your tiny garden, or a stinky camel in the street, so plastic models were fine. But when there'd been a request for "a real-live proper puppy that I can take for walks and will be my best friend" from Daisy McClean, she'd leaned in close and studied the freckled face and the quivering hopeful lip. Got her a small handful of dog biscuits and told her to pet the next dog she saw and ask if she could feed it the biscuits. So Daisy did, with her Dad, the next day in the park, and the dog she petted had pupped, and the owner was desperate to get them away – had talked to Missus

Lambert, actually, about putting up a notice. And her dad, soft-hearted man that he was, well – long story short, she got the puppy; a sweet, fluff of a thing. Still had it. Not so sweet these days, though. There'd been something, hadn't there? Something had happened, when they'd been older, 13 or so, not long after the Polo incident.

Daisy getting a dog started rumors that Missus Lambert was a witch, of sorts. Not impossible to believe even now, sat on hard wooden chairs while she sized them up. Laid out the rules. Stood up like a queen from her throne and beckoned them out of the cold light of the office, into the muggy dark of a storeroom so ill-lit that you couldn't tell what was shadows and what was shelving.

The shelves have a smell, that's the first thing they notice: above the dust, something sweet. And there's a well-worn trail through the dust straight down the middle of the room, barely lit by the faint yellow flickering bulb. The bulb hums as if there's flies trapped in it.

"Can't barely see nothing," says one of them.

"Sorry," says Missus Lambert briskly. She flicks a switch and the lights come on properly – flood-like along the walls. The shadows become the shelving, miles of it shelves, and refrigerators. The room's the size of a supermarket, a long one. It's 10, 50, 100 times bigger than the shop.

"How do you manage all this by yourself?" asks one – the one who stole.

Missus Lambert raises an eyebrow. "I won't be, will I, with you two delivering."

It's quite simple, she explains, leading them through a bewildering array of goods. She'll take the phone calls, the emails – *yes*, she snaps at the disbelieving expressions, the bitshop is online – and she will set the goods ready to deliver, and each day the boys will take the goods carefully house to house, as needed. And politely, for she'll not have the good name of the bitshop smirched by them. When they settle in, when it's clear they might be a good fit – though she says it strangely "if the shop fits you" – she'll allow them to fetch the goods themselves. She expects it won't take them long to learn their way around the stockroom ...

She stops at an arbitrary line.

"This, here onwards, is off-limits." Off-limits looks exactly like the bit of the room they're standing in, if the absolute end of it. There's a row of chest freezers against the back wall. They're filthy, finger marks on the edges where they've been opened, but otherwise thickly layered with dirt. The wall behind them bulges in a way that makes it look like it's moving, like one of those optical illusions. It's definitely warmer back here – the freezers must struggle.

Missus Lambert scuffs a mark on the floor. "You don't go beyond here. No matter what you come to get, you don't open those chests. I'll *know*."

"It's all right," they say to Mam when they get home. "She's not so bad."

"Well what sort of thing will you be delivering?" she says, plating up dinner. There's a swirling smell of warm grease and caramelized onions, and the chill of her anxiousness cuts through as though she didn't send them off to the job herself.

"Pork chops, today," says one, Michael, the one who stole. They're home now, and Mam can tell them apart even if no one else can. "Beans. Exciting things like that." Mam looks doubtfully at the chops on the plates she's just put on the table. Michael raises an eyebrow. "Perk of the job, Mam. It's *fine*."

"I delivered a new hat to someone," says the other, hurriedly – David. The one who pointed. He's not sure he'll be able to choke down a chop, 'cause Missus Lambert doesn't know about the perks Michael's decided to have. "Wouldn't have thought the bitshop was the place for clothes, but ..."

"And I delivered a box of pens."

"Nothing more than that, though?" asks Mam, a bit anxious. "Because Missus Lambert's a gem, of course, but some of the things people ask for …"

"What like?" says David, though he's not sure he wants to know what might really be lurking in that stockroom.

Mam laughs, a bit brittle. "Well, you know, there's rumors. Mr. Mudlam, that time, asked for something to make his wife happy, and then he vanished …"

"That one's just a joke, though," said David. "Everyone knows he had another family out in Helmingly-on-Sea."

"They haven't seen him either," said Michael. "That's what I heard. And anyway, she said not those things, not for delivery. So it's not a problem. Mam, what *are* you worrying about? You always worry."

"Oh," said Mam. "Just the Lamberts, they have long memories. It does well to stay on their right side."

"Oh, well, she definitely remembers us, if that's what you're worried about," says David. "And she still scares the shit out of me, like, but we'll be fine, if Michael behaves." He glares at his brother, who takes a big bite of pork chop and chews through his grin. "I think she might even like us. Likes that we're supporting the bitshop against evil corporations and all that bollocks, you know. Support your local independents."

"Language," says Mam, but so relieved that there's no strength to her admonishment.

Her sons make her a cup of tea, do the washing up. *They're well brought up*, she thinks. *That incident with the mints was the beginning and end of it.*

Pork chops, beans, weekly shops. Now that the shine of seeing behind the fly curtain is over, the best part of the job is the sneaking view into other people's lives. Mundane, mostly, but somehow fascinating to know that the fella at number 53 gets through about six bags of spinach a week; that her across the park needed a spindle for a spinning wheel (and Missus Lambert magicked one up). Word hasn't yet spread fully that the bitshop delivers, so a lot of the day involves standing around behind the counter, waiting for instructions, especially when both of them are working. It's been three weeks of delivering when David gets sent down to the storeroom by himself for the first time. Michael's out dropping off stationery, so David's alone with Missus Lambert, though he's pretty sure she doesn't know which twin he is.

Wellies, size 5 child. Blue, preferably.

"I'll draw you a map," she says. She draws him a map. "David, you'll be quite all right, I'm sure. Just keep your head."

It's a disconcerting sendoff for a task that, really, shouldn't be that difficult – both that he's supposed to keep his head, but also that she got his name right. Getting his name right means she's separating him from his brother – she's turning those truth-seeking eyes on him and they are working. And though it's frustrating being treated as one when they are two, there's also comfort in it: his brother's larger-than-lifeness is a shield to hide behind, and she has wiped that away.

And she knows it, he realizes. The stockroom is a test, of sorts, because he's noticed something, and she's noticed he'd noticed: they go *out* on delivery all the time, but Missus Lambert doesn't seem to get any stock delivered *in*.

In the little blue backroom, he has, again, that disconcerting moment of seeing his own back vanish into the dark beyond the curtain on the screen. He studies the map carefully – stupid, really, but suppose there's some code word for finding the wellies. Does Missus Lambert have other people living and working down there or something, smuggling goods in through a hidden doorway at the back? Maybe the rumors are real ...

The stockroom door swings open with its whispery little squeal. He catches it before it bangs into the wall, wipes his sweaty hands on his jeans and enters.

Can't find the light switch. Of course he can't – he was so busy gawping at the shelves first time round he never saw where they were. He pulls out his phone and turns on the torch function, casts the weak light around the walls. Nothing. It'll have to do.

It's not much better than the gray dark, all leaping shadow shapes, but at least he can count his way along the shelves and pull out a few wellies. He thinks of his brother, out in the bright sun, delivering sausages and A4 binders. They both still wear T-shirts to the shop. He has a feeling that the day they wear long sleeves, some sort of penance will have been paid, for an incident not even his fault.

1 – 2 – 3 – 4 – 5, left turn, right turn, four more shelves.

Here?

He wipes his hand along a shelf and raises a cloud of dust, peculiarly sweet and musty, like cedar mixed with honey. It huffs and snuffs up his nose till he sneezes - and the phone flies out of his hand and skitters under a shelf, almost as if it has a mind of its own. It skims the ground like some black-shelled bug running for its life, propelled by the glow of its belly. The dark is not pitch. It's worse than pitch – it's threateningly gray, lumpy, musty, draped with webs and cloths and the soft, flaking fingers of creatures that have never seen daylight.

David shudders, swears at himself for his imagination. Where *did* that thought come from? He remembers a trick Michael swore by when they were younger. Closes his eyes tight, stares at the back of his own eyelids and their panicked display of light splatters and floating orbs for what feels like full minutes. Actually opens them a few seconds later, braced for a world of gray.

Now he can see the faint outlines of the boxes and shelves. He feels his way along them carefully, until he's back to the middle aisle. At one end, so fine and glimmering it could be a mirage, is the outline of the door he came through. He will, he decides, admit defeat. Tell Missus Lambert that he's not ready for the secrets of the bitshop stockroom yet; he's a delivery boy, not a goods-fetcher. They are two different things, like he and Michael are two different people. Michael would make a great goods-fetcher – he does it naturally, not always legally. He doesn't get jumpy in the dark. But he, David, he's a delivery boy. He's good at giving, good at passing on. The only thing he is good at *taking*, he thinks sourly, is the blame for his brother's actions. His brother right now is out shagging Alice Emberly under the guise of delivering a packet of pens.

He shuffles carefully toward the rectangle, hands outstretched.

Michael would get a kick out of this, though, he thinks. And misses his brother for a second almost as much as he is angry with him.

The door doesn't seem to be getting any closer, so he walks faster, almost running, and he's nearly there, he thinks, nearly to the blue room where time feels a bit weird, but at least it doesn't smell, when he hears Missus Lambert calling him. He has just a moment to wonder why he can't see her in the doorway and why, also, she seems to be calling from behind him, before he trips against an obstacle, his toe catching under it, hurtling him forward over a sharp-edged corner which shoves the air out of him from the belly up and knocks his head briefly against old, painted stone.

He grabs on to the dark, trying to stay upright and smears his hands through the layers of dirt on the freezer chest he's landed on. The filth is soft under his fingers, like velvet. It occurs to him that freezers have lights – he need only open one and he will at least see where he is. There may even be a light switch at this end of the room – it would make sense, surely, for a room this long to have light switches at both ends, and especially if there was a door. He's sure there was a door; there was something ... He hooks his nails under the edge of the freezer and yanks against a long-closed seal. The whole freezer jerks, and then the lid releases with a hiss, and swings up loosely as if it's been waiting to open – as if it's been pushed from the inside.

There *is* light, and he's blinded for a moment by brilliance – and the smell. The awful smell. The freezer is broken, it must be, and whatever is inside, the colourful silhouettes, the neon outlines against the bright light – it is rotting. And he sees ... he sees ... reaching fingers, bare arms, roiled and tangled roots passing through and into a fleshy mound, a face, puckered and wrinkled, waking – mouth opening and closing in a yawn, and it turns its eyes to him and they are gimlets, lasering him, looking for guilt, looking for truth ...

Missus Lambert calls again, from somewhere far behind him, and the flood lights flare on.

He slams the lid closed.

It took him long minutes to shuffle the wrong way down the full length of the storeroom. It takes her seconds of angry stamping to reach the same place.

"Where are the wellies?" she demands. She places one hand flat on top of the chest freezer without looking down at it.

"I couldn't find the light switch," says David. "And I dropped my phone ..."

Missus Lambert nods, curtly, grabs him by the elbow and leads him first to the wellies, which are exactly where she said they would be, and then to the door, where she points at the light switches very obviously right next to the doorframe.

She unpurses her lips long enough to serve the welly-needing customer, and waits for the dooming jangle of the bell to fade before turning to David.

"And did you look, then?" she says, as casually as if they are carrying on a conversation from earlier. She is watching him the same way she must have watched Mrs. Selter when she asked for suitcases; when Mr. Mudlam asked for something to make his "bitch wife happy for once". And when Daisy McClean, David remembers now, when Daisy McClean asked for the dog who came to her rescue, mauling scars into the father who, it turned out, wasn't quite as soft as everyone thought.

He can't lie.

"Yeah," he says. "Missus Lambert, I don't think this job's for me."

"This shop's been here a long time," says Missus Lambert. "It keeps a balance. If you take you have to give; if you set roots you have to fertilize them. This shop's the roots of this town. Do you see what I'm saying?"

He doesn't.

"No," he says.

"Good," says Missus Lambert. She walks briskly – she walks so *briskly* for such an old lady – to the door of the shop and swings the sign closed. It is not yet time to close.

"You're not lying, that's good." David backs toward the crisps shelves. The packets crinkle into his back. Missus Lambert keeps coming, toward, toward … past. "You can't simply provide, you know. There's a balance, to making sure people get what they need, even if it's not what they want. You end up feeding yourself to a place like this, bit by bit. Body, soul, mind. It's wearing." She beckons him back over to the fly curtain, and he follows like a calf led by milk.

She points at the door, swinging gently open all by itself.

"It was for your own good, I told you stay away from it. It was an accident, I know, but we've got a taste of you now. So?"

"So," repeats David, dazed.

"So what do you want? Do you want to be out of a job, David? You're not the first I've had work here; you won't be the last. This is, as I said, a job of heart and soul. You'd be part of long tradition if you stayed. But if you choose not, you'd be the first I've had to let go."

David nods. "I know – we, we're probably not a good fit."

The door swings open wider. Out the front of the shop, the doorbell rings. Missus Lambert, hair neat, eyes twinkling and friendly now, looks at David with just a tilt of an eyebrow. "We, you say. Now, I don't know about *we*.

Hoi, now," she adds, "am I right that you would've had pork chops for dinner again the other night?"

David nods again.

Missus Lambert shakes her head. "Your Mam, she'll understand," she says. "You should go now. Consider this ... a redundancy. Not a firing."

On the little television screen, Michael pushes through the front door of the shop just as he pushes through the fly curtain, and he winks at David and grins at Missus Lambert and announces that he has a date with Alice, so he won't be working the Saturday. And Missus Lambert nods and smiles as though the dating lives of teenage boys are all she'd like to hear about, but her eyes are gimlets, and for now will Michael, please, fetch something from the stockroom for a delivery?

Michael grins – delighted – and punches David on the arm.

"Look at that – we're the inner circle now!" he says.

David daredn't punch him back. He doesn't want that to be the last thing he does to his brother. Missus Lambert gives Michael instructions, strict, and David's map. Michael pretty much skips into the stockroom, sticks his head back in, asks where the light switch is, and Missus Lambert shows him as if the lights will help him at all.

She settles in her armchair, presses a button on the TV and the scene changes.

David takes a wooden seat alone, and watches himself whistling through the stock room door, doing a jaunty walk down the middle aisle. Picking through the boxes, pocketing a thing or two. He watches himself hover at the line they were told not cross, and check back quick over his shoulder, and then step deliberately on toward the chest freezers, and when that happens he feels an icy shearing through his chest and his loses his breath for a second and goes dizzy.

He closes his eyes, and when he opens them, the screen has gone dark and Missus Lambert is gone, too, and the door to the storeroom is stood open. There's an envelope with "David" scrawled on it. and it's the pay he's owed, but he leaves it where it is, and hovers at the open door wondering whether it's too late to turn on the lights, and what he'll see if he does. He catches the smell of the open freezer, and hears a clattering of footsteps rushing out of the dark, and he hears a shriek that could be his own voice and as though caught on a string he turns and runs through the clinging tangle of the fly curtain. The curtain wraps his arms and catches in his hair and he thinks it's the curtain holding him and pulling him – he thinks it is, as he tears loose and runs home panting with tears streaming down his face. He runs home and it's just the one heart pounding, just the one person's breath gasping, just the one soul making it safe back.

Mam doesn't ask. She doesn't need to: sets the table for two, and tells her friends proudly that, yes, Michael's gone into retail: stockroom coordinator.

They still shop at the bitshop. Even knowing. Even then. They order an easy delivery once a month, but the parcels are left on the doorstep. No matter how David watches and waits at the window, he only ever sees his brother's back as he walks away, and Michael never turns around when David calls his name, and over the years one of them grows older and grayer and stoops and forgets which one he was, and the other has forgotten that he was ever two.

■

Francoise Harvey lives in the North East of England with her partner and an ancient husky. She has had stories published in The Dark, Black Static, Interzone, The Lonely Crowd, Litro, TSS (theshortstory.co.uk), Confingo *and others, as well as a standalone chapbook (Guest) published by Nightjar Press, and a story in* Best British Short Stories 2017 *(Salt, ed. Nicholas Royle) that was recently adapted for audio by* Cast of Wonders. *She is host of local magazine* NARC's My Writing Life *podcast, which means she gets to be nosy about how other writers write, and also works part-time in her local library.*

THE ANDROMEDA MAN

Gretchen Tessmer

"Aimee, is that you?" Aunt Vernie asks. The poor woman has classic mother-of-the-bride frazzling carved deep into her features. Her wrinkles are showing beneath the make-up. If she stands too close to a light switch, her hair might stand on end. It's nearly time for her only daughter's wedding ceremony, and all her last-minute checklists are still woefully incomplete.

Vernie always makes too many checklists. She sets herself up for failure.

Her arms are overflowing with bouquets of roses, sunflowers and baby's breath for six of Kasey's seven bridesmaids. The seventh bouquet is sitting in my lap, my fingers lazily picking at the cream-lace ribbons holding the stems together. I've picked out some of the baby's breath and set those white sprays on the little end table just beside me. I know it's a wedding, but there's no reason for so much baby's breath. It's choking out the flowers.

Vernie's late and headed down the hotel's stairwell at a rushed pace. She stops short when she catches sight of Gram and me, hanging out in a cozy lounge area by the 4th floor elevators. She says again, more insistently this time, "Aimee?"

"Yes, we're here," I answer, a little reluctantly. Since grabbing breakfast in the café downstairs, I've been enjoying a quiet interlude with Gram, feeling a little like maybe I belong at this thing, after all. With a last-minute, phoned-in invite from Vernie, "What? You never got your save-the-date? The post office is so unreliable these days." I'd spent most of the drive up to Tremblant feeling like the alien cousin three-times-removed.

Guests dressed in pressed suits and fancy gowns, waistcoats and bow ties, sparkly jewels and patent leather heels, have been filtering through the hallway for the better part of an hour, mulling around, all on their way downstairs, to take their seats on the sunny veranda where the string quartet is already plucking out the first notes of *Le Cygne* and Kasey's husband-to-be is currently joking around with his groomsmen, laughing with approval as the boys rate the bridesmaids on a scale of one to ten. At least, that's what they were doing when I went downstairs half an hour ago to give that pack of frat boys a box of boutonnieres.

"Why aren't you and Grandma downstairs?" Vernie demands, her tone as pinched as her expression, groaning at her own short-sightedness in thinking she had everything under control. She's a tight wire, ready to snap. "We're starting in fifteen minutes!"

I shrug innocently and tip my head toward the old woman in the chair beside me. What can I say? At Gram's insistence, we're waiting for the Andromeda Man to show up. My Gram is incredibly stubborn, always has been, and won't be told what to do. Vernie should know this. She was raised by Gram, too.

And it's not like she's never heard Gram talk about the Andromeda Man before. Sure, Gram keeps the more absurd references light with everybody else, even Kasey … but not with Vernie and certainly not with me. I take it as a compliment. But not Vernie. At best, she finds Gram's delusions inconvenient. At worst, she thinks her mother is doing this on purpose, ever trying to sabotage her *entire* life.

She moved to Montréal when she turned eighteen and hasn't looked back since. She rolls her eyes whenever her mother starts talking this way, and she blames me for indulging the silly conte de fées, I'm sure.

Because I do. Or at least, I don't fight Gram on it. Which, to Vernie, is basically the same thing.

"We'll be down soon, chère, but we can't expect the Andromeda Man to find his way to your daughter's wedding alone, n'est-ce pas?" For Vernie's benefit, Gram tweaks her reasons for waiting on our mysterious and long-awaited guest. She admitted to me earlier that the whole point of getting him here is to ditch this charade completely.

Oh, Gram …

Gram will be 93 next month, but that's not really an excuse. Her mind's still as sharp as a needle. And she's more of a spitfire now than she's ever been, still claiming the title of family matriarch by a long mile, much to Vernie's eternal chagrin. But she's been talking about the Andromeda Man since I was a little girl. I've always assumed it's a mangling of some old Acadian saying that I don't know or referencing a speck of village somewhere in France, lost in translation. She would refer to him like Santa Claus or St. Christopher, as in "best eat your vegetables, chère, or the Andromeda Man will be disappointed in you" or "remember the Andromeda Man in your prayers." I thought maybe it was a joke.

But lately, she's been leaning into it more literally. She's convinced he's coming this time. Here, today, beside the 4th floor elevators in this solidly 3-and-1/2 star

Marriott Hotel, with all its polyester bedspreads, nylon carpets and sedate, pastel-colored still lifes.

But I love Gram. It was just the two of us for such a long time. She raised me in her little pink cottage in the Laurentians, with maple syrup on blueberry pancakes, jugs of apple cider lining the cellar each fall, and runaway flower gardens rivaling whatever blooms they have in Marché de Vieux-Port. My mother died early. Too early. And I've never met my father. I don't know if he's dead, too, or just a plain deadbeat.

Gram's all I have. So, if she wants to sit by the elevators and wait for an elusive Andromeda Man to make some glorious appearance, that's where we'll sit.

Anyway, for all her long-suffering sighs, Vernie's just as delusional, if on a different level. I've met Kasey's groom. Several times now. He's awful. There's no question. I'm not just saying that. He's hit on me twice in the last forty-eight hours and he hasn't been subtle about it.

Hey, anyone ever tell you that your eyes are like fucking stars?

Yeah, a couple times. I've gotten long looks my whole life. And if that's all he said, without the booze-influenced follow-up asking if I wanted to see his room—"the groom's room," he winked—I wouldn't have been offended. But if this marriage lasts more than three months ... well, good for them. I'm not holding my breath.

And I'm not holding so much baby's breath either … I pull a few more sprigs.

"Maman, come on," Vernie insists, begs, pleads, gestures with her chin. Her eyes are rolling to high heaven. "Kasey needs us downstairs *now*."

Gram shakes her head firmly, and I just stay out of it. Why does Vernie think she'll get her way in this? Still, I mouth the word "sorry" to Vernie after Gram's gaze returns to the elevator, as a sort of peace offering. I can sympathize with my aunt. It's a big day for her, mother-of-the-bride and all that. I get it. If I had any power to sway Gram and get her downstairs, I'd use it, je promets. But I don't.

Neither of us do, Vernie. So just give it a minute, okay?

Vernie doesn't buy my apology. She never does. She thinks I'm doing this on purpose. Her glare is icy as she disappears down the stairwell with the bouquets. Here's hoping the girls downstairs take scissors to those generous sprays of baby's breath before they head out down the aisle.

"Sometimes, I hate that woman," Gram mutters as soon as Vernie's gone. She's dressed up in grandmother-of-the-bride best, with pearl earrings and a velvet cloche hat that my grandfather bought her in Paris, on his way back from fighting the Nazis. Her gnarled fingers are wrapped in her favorite rosary, counting out its glass beads.

"Gram …," I chide her, if lightly. I'm seven decades too young to scold her. And I'm in no mood for it anyway, relaxed, my high heels abandoned to the carpet, my feet pulled up under me. Still, I remind her, "She's your daughter."

"Véronique's insufferable," Gram replies. "Your mother was never that way and neither are you, chère. I don't know where she gets it. Look at these bridesmaids' dresses she's chosen …"

She gestures at the olive-green gown I'm wearing, reaching out to touch the fabric at my shoulder. She scrunches up her wrinkled face, adding solemn lines to the deep creases already there.

"It's chiffon, Gram. Vernie says it's classic."

"She might as well have gone with fishing net. It clashes with your eyes."

This isn't Vernie's fault. My eyes are colored like labradorite—blue, gray, green and violet mixed and tossed together like seas in stormy weather or rainbows bursting into pieces. Or, apparently, *like fucking stars*. My eyes clash with everything.

As do I, it seems.

Last night, after three grape-flavored vodka martinis, Kasey came over to where I was leaning on the bar, draped her arm around my shoulder as if we're the kind of cousins who talk more than once every ten years and told me bluntly, "You know that Mom put you in my wedding just to make Grandma happy, right? Grandma said she wouldn't come otherwise and Mom didn't want everyone speculating on our family drama."

She didn't need to say it. I'm well aware that once Gram is gone, my invites to family functions will cease. Sometimes blood is no thicker than paint thinner.

"Should we head downstairs?" I ask Gram, gently attempting a change of scenery. We've been waiting for the Andromeda Man for an hour now. Not surprisingly, no one's shown up.

"No, my sweet, not yet," Gram shakes her head firmly. "He'll be here. I sent for him this time."

We listen to the calm hum of elevators moving through upper floors. Changing subjects, she wonders, "I thought you were bringing a young man to this thing?"

"Who—Marc?" I laugh, a little dryly. "No, he couldn't make it. He's been playing accordion in a post-punk-whatever band this semester and they have a gig tonight that pays in drinks so ... yeah, I think I'm breaking up with him."

"Good," Gram approves. "Don't waste your time, mon coeur. The men on Earth aren't good enough for you. You're like your mother that way."

"How's that?"

"She always loved her Andromeda Man. It was those eyes. Les yeux pleins d'étoiles."

Les yeux pleins d'étoiles. Star eyes.

"Wait … the Andromeda Man knew my mother?" I smirk, amused at this newest twist in an old, old story.

"Bien sûr," Gram replies, patiently. "If your mother didn't know your father, chèrie, how would you be here?"

I blanch a little, only because she seems so serious. And we never talk about my father. Not ever. I don't even know his name. He's as foreign to me as …

At that moment, the elevator bell dings and the doors open with a shudder.

"Oh, Dieu merci," Gram sighs with relief, crossing herself. A man exits the elevator—tall, middle-aged, his black hair streaked with liberal amounts of gray. He could be anyone.

"Hello, Yvette," he greets my grandmother at once, without hesitation, reaching down and squeezing her palm gently. She beckons him down with her other hand, those rosary beads still laced between her fingers. He apologizes in an accent that's hard to place, "Sorry I'm late."

"You had a long way to come." She touches his cheek with affection, spilling apologies of her own, "I never meant to keep her from you. That was my mistake, but

I couldn't give up my petite-fille. Not after we lost her mother."

Gram glances at me. The man, whoever he is, wherever he's from, looks at me too. I find myself face-to-face with eyes the same strange color as my own—blue, gray, violet and green. The color of storms, seas and stars bursting into pieces.

My father's eyes.

So, turns out, I was more the *half*-alien cousin three times removed.

We don't make it to Kasey's wedding. *Quel dommage*, as Gram would say. And I'm sure Aunt Vernie will have plenty to say on the subject too, the next time I see her ... which, honestly, might not be for a while.

Gram did mangle one thing in translation—the Andromeda Man hails from much farther away than the galaxy next door.

◾

Gretchen Tessmer is a writer based in the U.S./Canadian borderlands. She writes both short fiction and poetry, with work appearing in over fifty publications, including Nature, Strange Horizons, Beneath Ceaseless Skies, Asimov's *and* F&SF, *as well as previous appearances in* Bourbon Penn.

NINE RECORDINGS OF GRIEF

Zachariah Claypole White

Tape #1

Hi, Aide. It's me.

Wow. What a stupid way to start. Not like you're going to hear this.

●

Listen. It's all coming to an end—everything. I'll try to get as far as the mountains, assuming the gas holds out. That seems as good a place as any. I mean, some of those caves run miles deep. Maybe I could …

●

What am I saying? Nature was your thing, Aide. Not mine. I just sit around writing ghost stories and reading Heidegger. Oh—by the way: ontology seems even more pointless during the apocalypse.

And there's that word.

•

I'll get to the mountains, okay? And then—well, one crisis at a time, right? I guess you taught me something after all.

•

I'm sorry, babe. I know this doesn't make much sense, but I'm doing my best, okay? Trying to explain how it's all unraveling. Trying to be honest. Like I promised you I would. I guess even then it was too late.

•

The world ended three days ago, and I've been driving ever since. I know. I should be out of gas by now. Sometimes nothing changes for hours. The trees are scorched bare; there's no wind anymore. Maybe all that's left are photos of the dead earth, tossed up against the windshield. Sometimes I check the speedometer just to prove the car's actually moving. Sometimes the horizon bulges and twists like cling film wrapped across a hurricane.

Hearing myself say that ... Maybe I'm losing my mind. Ya think so?

•

But I've seen Them, Aide. Not sure how to make you understand. They don't move right. You ever see a centipede cut in half? That frenzy of legs? Each one squirming in its own direction? They move like that, the things that ate the sky. They move like they're going through the world. Not touching it but pushing us, and everything else, out the way.

•

Wait, did I say three days? No, it's only been one. One day since the world ended. One. Details matter, right? The sun has come up twice though. Of course, that might not be the sun.

•

I wish I could hear you laugh again, Aide. I know that sounds stupid. Especially when I'm driving through a literal hell, but you had the best laugh—especially your giggle. It was the first thing I loved about you. Did I ever tell you that? Aide?

Tape #2

Should have mentioned it sooner, but it's only me in this cramped Subaru. Mel got out when we hit the state line— what was left of it anyway. The tarmac had blistered and split open like a cicada shell. Leaves melted down from the branches. And across the highway... I can't think about it, Aide. Just can't.

•

Okay, fine. I did say I'd try. Didn't I? You can't look at Them for too long. But you get these glimpses: angles that can't exist; something like an eel or angler fish, bigger than any ocean; translucent clouds—all veins and tendons—watching you with your mother's eyes.

•

Wait, was I telling you about Mel? Since we left the city it's been harder to think straight. But Mel—who laughed at every stupid pun, who slept on my floor for three days after you died—she's gone now.

She was singing before she left.

It started after we crossed into Virginia, a kind of whining hum. I thought it was the muffler. Then I saw her staring at me, mouth pressed shut, trying to hold back that noise. But she couldn't. Her lips burst open and the song poured out. I've never heard anything like it, Aide. Imagine a forest's worth of spring peepers, mid-tune, shoved through a meat grinder.

I pulled over, begged her to stop, even tried to force her jaw shut, but every muscle in her body was locked in place. Except for her tongue. The way it kept moving, Aide—oh God—like a horse caught in barbed wire.

Then I must have blacked out, because the next thing I remember was Mel closing the passenger door. And the noise had stopped. She seemed back to her old self. I begged her not to leave; told her we'd be safer together.

She shook her head, said something about going home. I tried to explain we were hours from her folks' house; that we'd agreed the mountains would be our best—and only— shot. But she'd already turned away. The singing started again.

•

I should have called you sooner, babe. Even after the fight. I should have known to check in. I should have noticed. I should have, should have, should ...

Tape #3

Mel left her tape recorder behind: the vintage one she got with a box of cassettes at some flea market outside the city. You know how Mel loved her old-timey shit. Fuck. No. I meant, how she loves. *Loves*. She may be the world's worst singer, but she's not dead. I didn't mean to say that.

Anyway, that's what I'm leaving these messages on. Jazz mixtapes from the eighties! Can you believe it? I think she knew what I'd use them for ... that I'd want to talk to you, in whatever way I could.

•

There's not much left, Aide. Of the sky, I mean. That first night, it just fell away. Like skin from an open wrist. And behind it—that's where They come from. The place we'll all end up. Bulbous, scuttling towers, like anemones.

Or deep-sea vents. Or maggots on roadkill. You don't want to look, you try not to, but Christ, it's beautiful. Beautiful in a way that makes you want to open up your veins—just to see that impossible place reflected in some small, leaking part of you.

•

Did you see it before the rest of us, Aide? All those months ago? Maybe you caught a glimpse and decided to beat the rush.

•

Mel kept asking, why now? Why us? Hell, They could have been chewing away at existence for decades—centuries. Or maybe They figured the stars had aligned. Oh, the stars have gone too, if you're interested.

I've had a lot of time to think it over. Not much else to do sitting in this goddamn car. Know what I realized? You know what genius, apocalypse-solving conclusion I reached? It doesn't fucking matter. Trying to understand why or what They are would be like a gnat trying to make sense of a mushroom cloud.

TAPE #4

Aidan, I don't want to talk about the fight ...

Mel told me you would have done it regardless. Even if I hadn't been such an asshole. I never believed her. Now though—at the end—I think I do.

But I keep wondering—after you made the cuts—did you replay that stupid, fucking fight? Was that your last thought of me? Or worse, what if you didn't think of me at all?

•

See? You were right. Even now I'm a selfish bastard.

•

Hey. You remember the storm door at your mom's place? How one day her lawnmower shot a rock right through it, but the glass still hung there, waiting for someone to touch the handle and bring it all crashing down? That's the world now, Aide. The rock's been thrown, and I'm waiting to see who finally opens the door.

•

They're getting closer. And bringing that other place with Them. Look how the towers move—like swarms of jellyfish.

•

It's an awful thing to say, but I wish you were here. Yep. Still selfish.

Tape #5

And you are! Here I mean—in the car. I know you can't be, but you're with me. Were you always so thin? I can hear you laughing. Laughing over the radio, laughing through the new dark. Laughing through my own mouth.

We could stay like this. Wait for it all to end. Even if you aren't really you, it would be enough.

•

Oh, Christ. Your wrists. Why is there so much blood? Please. Let me help. Why won't it stop, Aide? Why won't the bleeding stop?

Tape #6

Hey, at least the gas is holding out. And the radio works again. Want to hear? Of course you do.

•

No, Aide. You have to listen, really listen, damnit. That's your problem—you never fucking listen. Not to Mel, not to your mom, and God forbid, certainly not to me. No, never me. You'd rather get intimate with a kitchen knife than ask for my help. Isn't that right, you selfish piece of shit?

•

I'm going to dig you up and kill you again, Aidan. I'll hollow out your bones with that same knife and let the new world pour in. I'll cut away those tidy little stiches till your hands come off easy as a lizard's tail. I'm going to curl up nice and warm inside your beautiful chest. Pour myself a glass of Bulleit and watch this whole fucking world come apart.

•

Can you hear it now?

•

Are you listening?

•

Aidan?

Tape #7

Babe, I'm so sorry. I didn't mean it. I don't remember saying any of that. The car's idling on the shoulder and the parking brake's on. I must have passed out again. That wasn't me. I swear.

•

I tried to erase the tape. The one where I went batshit with a capital B. But there's a noise on it, a melody—the one Mel was singing. As soon as I reached for the cassette, I heard it. Just listening to the tape rewind made me puke my guts out. If I hear it again, I think I'll stop being me. I'll walk out of this car and keep going till I'm somewhere else. Like Mel.

•

Oh yeah, and the Subaru smells of the world's worst hangover. So far, the apocalypse is going just great, thanks for asking.

•

Aide, where'd you go? It's dark now; all the light has slipped beyond.

•

Please come back. I don't want to die alone.

Tape #8

Well, that's it. Out of gas. I had a full tank when Mel and I left, but that was seven days ago. Yeah, I know—even your hybrid couldn't run for a week straight, but time doesn't hold much weight anymore. This happened yesterday; it'll also happen tomorrow.

•

It's weird, kinda funny almost, but I haven't been this calm since you died. Everything's gone still, you know? You'd probably say I'm in shock. Then you'd quote some study about trauma response in nurses and then you'd say... you'd say...

You've probably figured it out by now, but I'm not going to reach the mountains. Even if I could it wouldn't make a difference. I can see flashes of Them, crawling across the peaks.

It's alright though. I'm alright.

I'm going to keep talking. Okay? At least for a while. Until I get there, wherever it is you went, wherever it is we're all going. Maybe I'll see you.

•

Just once more.

TAPE #9

The sky's finally gone. All of it. Everything's brighter, though. Don't even need the headlights. I was right, it is beautiful. Writhing towers of coral and bone twitch in the dead air, waiting for new tenants. Some of the monoliths reach for one another, desperate for touch. I can hear Them. Like insects covering a window pane. All those legs clicking and clicking and clicking ...

There are people around the base of each tower. It's hard to tell from here, but something—a vine, a spiderweb—is sprouting out of them. Out of their ears and throats. They're gagging and screaming and sobbing and everyone is singing.

•

It's almost time to leave, Aide. Mel's walking down the road toward me. I know it's not really her. Maybe she's one last gift from my exhausted sanity. But when she gets here, I'll have to follow. I hope you understand.

•

There's someone with her—someone so familiar.

•

I love you, Aide. Even now that has to mean something. It might make me a shit person, but I miss you so much more than the world.

■

Zachariah Claypole White is a Philadelphia-based writer and educator, originally from North Carolina. He holds a BA from Oberlin College and an MFA from Sarah Lawrence College, where he was a Jane Cooper Poetry Fellow. His poetry and prose have appeared in or are forthcoming from Southeast Review, Weird Horror, *and* The Rumpus, *amongst others. Zachariah has received support from the* Kenyon Review *Writers Workshop and his awards include* Flying South's *2021 Best in Category for poetry as well as nominations for a Pushcart Prize and Best of the Net. Zachariah teaches at the Community College of Philadelphia and the Writing Institute at Sarah Lawrence College.*

THE BLACK HOLE

Adriane Hanson

Rye tipped his head back, exposing the stubbled bark of his throat, raw from razor burn.

"Mi corazón es una boca," he said, exhaling a cloud of smoke.

I sat on the windowsill and flexed my feet, the oil-black polish on my toes shimmering in the sun. Rye lay on the porch roof, below my reach, reading a book of Mexican poetry and sucking on a shriveled joint.

I took a sip of the slushy Rye had made. Blue Gatorade, Robotussin and crushed ice. When I stirred the drink, it turned queasy purple. *Yuck.* I took another few sips for luck.

Growls rose from the basement of the house next door, then the throb of bass guitar. Sirens whooped far off in the distance. Drunks and dogs howled. A train rattled over the tracks down the block. From my perch, I could see the hopper cars shrieking by, loaded with coal and decorated with graffiti: yellow fangs dripping blue blood, CORPSE PARTY spelled in acid green bubble letters, a hot-pink rat king devouring itself.

I was hoping for a storm, but the evening was clear and hot. A mosquito flew in lazy circles before landing on Rye's naked chest. On cooler days I loved to run my fingers through the carpet of wiry blond hairs. He reached up and smacked himself, leaving a dark streak of blood.

At the beginning of the summer, we had planned to apply for scholarships to study in Mexico next year, it would even count toward Rye's Spanish literature major, but in the last few weeks all of our motivation seemed to have dissolved into the humid air. Rye lost his job as a dishwasher just as our first month's rent on the room was due. Too many times he snuck down to the river instead of showing up for his shift. Now he collected cans, donated his plasma, did odd jobs for our friends, but the bills were still mostly up to me. We'd agreed that he'd find another job once he was stable enough.

"Siempre tengo hambre," said Rye. "Pero nunca satisfecho."

Jared, the guy who owned the house, kept the candles lit and the curtains shut most evenings, his prayer circle gathered around the living room table, so we were confined to the hotter second floor. Amens and muted pleas rose up through the wood and carpet. Many afternoons the drone lulled me to nap, but my shift at the bar started in ten. Rye's eyes shut. The medicine he took made him sleepy all the time, nearly impossible to wake.

I turned and lowered myself onto the bedroom floor. The dun-colored carpet was crusted with stains, streaked with neon colors where I'd spilled my polish. Laundry consumed most of the room. The pile breathed, expanding and contracting in the sticky heat of the house. Empty film canisters rolled across the floor when I shut the window. I found my black miniskirt and a clean-enough black T-shirt and slipped them on.

"Rye!" I yelled down to him. No response.

Watching his chest rise and fall, his eyes scanning some interior horizon, I remembered the winter when we were first together, waking up in his bed most mornings under the stained plaid comforter, the warmth of his body surrounding me. Even in the winter he was a furnace. Wet clumps of snow slid down the windows. He'd tell me his dreams, whole lifetimes, and it was like we were the only people in the universe. I rarely remembered my own dreams.

Another mosquito landed on his eyelid, feeding on a faint purple river. Rye was alive. He'd probably be alive when I came back. I rested my chin on the windowsill. Maybe I wouldn't come back.

As I walked past the sugar beet refinery, smell like corn burning the air, I imagined grains sifting into my lungs, sweetness dissolving in the warmth of my blood. I kept my eyes down. The only things to see were metal towers thrusting into hot gray sky, smoke billowing from their mouths, and grass burned colorless by the sun.

The Bar at the End of the World was a one-story brick building at the edge of our neighborhood. The building was once a butcher's shop; the concrete floor was still stained with faded blood by the drains. A mural of a mushroom cloud decorated the back wall above the pool tables, and a TV played a continuous mute loop of old sci-fi movies.

Sean was wiping down the bar, rubbing the gleaming wood in slow, methodical circles. I stood outside for a moment watching him, his auburn hair inflamed by evening light, the shops across the road reflected in the glass storefront, Rainbow Liquors and Daddy O's Guns 'n' More, its red sign blinking *Pawn Pawn Pawn*. I lifted my hands and made a box with my thumbs and index fingers, like I was taking a photograph. *Click.* I needed to get my camera fixed, but that would take time and money.

One of our regulars, Roger, sat at the end of the bar nursing a whiskey. He lived in the low-income housing units across from the refinery and wore a red and black poncho despite the heat. Otherwise, the bar was empty. Even on the busiest days Sean never seemed rushed or stressed. His arms were strong and freckled, his eyes chips of granite. I wanted to turn around and run home.

Sean didn't look up when I opened the door.

"Sarah," he said. "You're late."

I looked around the room. Roger raised his glass and grunted a hello.

"Sorry to leave you alone with the thirsty throngs."

Sean finally raised his eyes to mine. "Punctuality is important," he said.

"Thanks for the advice," I mumbled, but I couldn't commit to the sarcasm.

As I walked behind the bar and put my purse on top of the icemaker, I pictured myself laying on the bed of ice, curled like a shrimp, slick and blue veined, Sean closing the door and latching it. He'd love to hear me plead to be let out.

Sean ghosted past me. Wrung out the dirty red rag in the sink.

"I'm going to do inventory," he said, bending down and opening the trap door, descending into the basement storage room. He turned on the light and closed the door behind him.

I checked the levels of the well bottles in the metal shelf below the bar. The altar of expensive booze behind me, lit up by red Christmas lights, was mostly for show. The garnish trays were all full, the lemons, limes and oranges cut into uniform slices, in the precise and infuriating way Sean did everything. I wondered sometimes what had gone wrong in his life for him to wash up here.

I clenched and unclenched my fists.

Smile, my mother's voice admonished me. *No one likes a sulky girl.* The voice was losing power. Eventually, with enough time and distance, I'd send it down into oblivion. I needed to make at least $300 this weekend to take care of our bills.

"How's it hanging, doll?" Roger asked.

"*Asi-asi.* How are you?"

Sean had told me that Roger would be 93 on his next birthday, but I wasn't sure if I believed him. "I'm fine," he said, "Except ...."

I topped off his Jack and poured myself a shot. We clinked glasses, giggling.

"Except?" I prompted him.

"Except ... oh what the devil do you call them? The others ... they keep trying to get into the house. Every summer, they come back. I put that poison around the perimeter of the wall, but they still keep coming."

"The others?"

"Oh you know ... the bugs, the insects, umm ... ants! Ants! HA!" He slapped the bar.

"Ants?"

"With any luck they'll eat me before my kids can put me in a home. Before I start shitting myself and drooling like a goddamned infant."

"That would take a lot of ants."

"I'll cover myself in honey and leave the door open," Roger said. "Eventually something will come in and eat me."

His gnarled hand clenched the glass. He gulped the rest of the whiskey and gestured for more. A Post-it below the bar listed his daughter's number, for nights when he got too twisted.

On the television screen an astronaut wheeled head over heels toward a black hole, a glut of random objects hurtling with him: a refrigerator decorated with clumps of magnetized letters, a mounted deer head, a fire extinguisher, a pink five-pound weight. The astronaut's face could not be seen; his helmet reflected the corona of flame around the black hole.

The door creaked open. I smelled the group of men before I saw them: lawn clippings, sweat and curdled milk.

"Hey ma," Jorge said to me, "Seven shots of your finest rail whiskey please. What a scorcher."

Jorge owned a landscaping business that serviced rich clients in the suburbs. I liked him because he talked like a sailor and tipped like a prince.

My stomach dropped as I stepped on the trapdoor to grab extra shot glasses. I turned to put them on the bar and poured down the line without losing a drop.

"How's school going?" Jorge asked me.

I shrugged. "It's summer."

After I moved in with Rye, my parents cut me off. They said that was the "last straw." Seemed to me they'd had plenty of last straws before, so I don't know what made this the *last* last straw. Maybe because I cursed them out, salted the earth behind me. They thought Rye was the one thing standing between me and a normal, settled life, the type of material accomplishments they could brag about to their friends. My mother wanted me to change my major from photography to something more practical, and truth was she probably wasn't wrong. What was I going to do, photograph weddings? Spend my life documenting other people's happiness? Bartending paid better, but not enough to support two people. I had two years left in school and Rye had two and a half. I was only 23, but the gap between where I was and where I was supposed to be felt insurmountable.

The men clinked their glasses and downed the whiskey in a chorus of grunts.

Roger rapped his knuckles on the bar and I topped him off. I tried not to think of Sean moving around downstairs, fingers caressing the bottles as he counted them. I knew he would come up and help if things got too busy, but he'd rather be alone with his carefully stacked crates. He liked things that were easy to master. Sean spent the first week I worked at the bar testing me relentlessly, asking me to make obscure drinks that no one would ever order, Brandy Alexanders and Manhattans, watching me with wasp eyes as the bar filled up to see if I'd lose my cool. Lately he had let up a bit, but he still watched me closely, forever making a list of my inadequacies in his head.

It was a busy night, but everyone cleared out by twelve. I stood counting my tips, putting the ones back into the register and exchanging them for twenties. I stuck the wad into my purse. Not bad for a Thursday. Sean turned off the open sign, brushed past me and opened the trap door. He disappeared into the basement.

I hesitated at the top of the stairs. *I really should go home.* The wheels of the midnight train shrieked against polished tracks, tracks that crisscrossed the nation and beyond, flat across deserts and prairie, raveling through the mountains, under and through neon cities, millions of columns of light blazing in the blackness. I smoothed my hair and followed Sean down into the dark.

The porchlight was off. Of course. I always asked Rye to leave it on and he always forgot. I picked my way carefully across the broken pavement and up to the door. I used my cellphone for light as I struggled to get the key in. Sean's cum still dripped out of me.

I wondered if I would get pregnant. The first time we had sex, Sean asked me if I was on the pill and I nodded, even though I'd gone off months before and hadn't gotten around to getting a new prescription. Rye and I didn't fuck all that much, the medicine put a damper on his libido, and he always pulled out when we did. I could have asked Sean to wear a condom, but I was convinced that talking about what we were doing would destroy the strange magic, break the spell we were under. We never spoke about it, or drifted outside of the roles we'd established in the beginning. I tried not to think about the things we did in the basement, the red wave that broke over me whenever he touched me.

Finally, the key fit into the lock and I opened the door. The inside of the house was darker and hotter than outside. It smelled like incense and stale pizza. I groped my way through the living room and up the stairs.

Light glowed at the end of the hall. Rye was passed out across the bed, arms akimbo, the lamp still on. Heat radiated from his body. I could feel it even across the room, his sweaty bulk. The gravity of his body pulling me toward him.

When you fall into a black hole, there's something called the event horizon, a line you cross after which there is no escape. Your body will stretch and stretch until you're ripped apart. It used to comfort me to think of black holes, to imagine being pulled apart by the hot dark, every atom obliterated. There are 100 million black holes in our galaxy alone. All those vortexes ready to suck you in.

Papers and books were scattered across the floor, a half-eaten piece of cake, smears of blue frosting on the carpet, an almost-empty bottle of codeine cough syrup prescribed to Jared. Taking off my clothes, I threw myself down on the bed next to him, drank the rest of the codeine, then turned off the light.

Sean's freckled hands, cupping my breasts, tracing my ribs, squeezing tighter and tighter around my neck. The only light his cellphone across the room, someone trying to contact him. Bottles jutted against each other as he thrust into me. His fingers in my mouth tasted like bleach. I put my hands on Rye's soft belly and banished Sean, tried to banish Sean. Eventually, my heartbeat slowed, my breath syncing up with Rye's snores. The dark infinite enclosed me.

I opened my eyes and the darkness resolved into shadows, the shapes of our bedroom. There was a low crackle, like corn popping, coming from outside. The sound had woken me up.

Rye snored beside me. I sat up and crept to the window, pulling aside the corner of the curtain. The streetlight closest to us was out.

A man shuffled down the center of the street. I blinked, rubbed my fists into my eyes. The man was on fire. He walked slowly, the flames that licked him from head to toe seeming to cause him no pain. Bright against the darkness of the road, he left his own afterimage behind him.

I couldn't move. *I'm dreaming.* The man passed in front of our house. *I must be dreaming.* I wanted to go hide under the covers, but I was rooted to the floor.

There was something familiar about the way he moved, but I couldn't make out his face. Suddenly he stopped and his head jerked toward our house. I fell backward, knocking over a tower of books, scrambled up against the wall and crouched under the window-ledge, trembling.

Rye turned over in his sleep with a grumble. Paralyzed, I tried to call his name, but nothing came out. Slowly, slowly, I lifted the edge of the curtain. The street was deserted and dark.

I turned on the lamp, looked at all the ordinary things in our bedroom: the clock with the golden arms that always showed the wrong time, books on the sagging shelf, Rye's chest rising and falling. I crawled in next to him, letting the clammy heat of his body lull me back to sleep.

• • •

Before we got our room in Jared's house, Rye and I had been living like stray cats, crashing at friends' houses or down by the river, where at night, train kids and local bums would gather around a bonfire passing bottles. Anything to avoid going home to our parents' houses. Rye got along with the homeless, the burnouts and the oogles. Like dogs, they sensed one of their own. I'd always be on the outside, no matter how many nights I slept rough. If it was cold enough, I'd slink back to my family's house, sneaking in after everyone was asleep, raiding the pantry and leaving before my parents woke in the morning.

During the day the river depressed me. Trash curdled the banks and collected on the beach, strangling the tree-roots. Eddies of suspicious-looking foam surged with debris. It was too polluted to swim in but people still did. At night though, the water flowed quicksilver, mysterious, the sounds of the current would lull me to sleep no matter how uncomfortable I was in the dirty sand or stuffed into someone's unwashed sleeping bag. If I had cash on me, I kept it in my underwear.

Rye and I grew up in the same neighborhood, a block apart. In elementary school, Rye and his friends would spy on me, hiding in the bushes that surrounded my family's sunroom. I would hear them giggling and suddenly get self-conscious. All I could see was a quiver in the leaves but I knew they were watching me, and everything I did became a performance. The way I walked across the carpet, dipped my paintbrush in pools of color, turned the pages in my books. I could never relax when they were out there. It came back to me when I started working for Sean, that creepy-crawly sensation of always being on display, a thing to be judged and picked apart.

Rye and I would play with the other neighborhood kids, flashlight tag on summer nights, sardines in Misty Monroe's house, the largest on the block, all of us stuck close together under beds and in cupboards. It was one of those times, when Rye was the hider and I was the first to find him, that we had our first kiss, under a blue tarp in the garage, the wheel of Mr. Monroe's motorcycle digging into my back. Afterward, we avoided each other for months. In the winter Mr. Monroe would attach a kayak to the back of his truck and pull us all through the snow, going faster and faster until my hair streamed behind me and the wind wrenched a scream from my throat.

My family was typical: silent resentment and occasional peaks of anger. My mother pick, pick, picking at the two of us, my father flayed and penitent. But Rye's was different. His dad looked just like him, the same blond stubble and milky blue eyes. Beer always in hand, he had nursed a middle-aged paunch since I could remember. By the time we were in high school he had graduated to liquor and was slowly drinking himself to death, cursing the wife who had abandoned him, his feckless son and anyone else who had the misfortune of coming across him. He liked to pinch my thighs, dig his thumb into the dip of my knee, like he was testing to see if I was ripe.

So, you can imagine how well he reacted when Rye started acting erratically junior year, when our English teacher found him kneeled on the moat of stones that bordered the school, hands bloodied, digging frantically in the sand below the rocks. He said he could hear a baby crying down there. By then we were a real couple. Rye's dad scoffed at the idea that his son's problems were anything other than acting out. When Rye would disappear, sometimes for days, off hopping trains or fuck knows, and come back filthy, claiming not to remember where he'd been, eyes hollowed out and replaced with glass, his father would act like he had been on some frolicsome adolescent adventure, put him in a headlock and call him a scoundrel. Rye never had a chance with or without me, that's the terrible truth, but I might have had a chance without him.

• • •

"This guy says you can get infected by ghosts from eating bad meat."

"What?"

"Like spirits are a parasite."

Rye raised the book he was reading. *Mundo de los espíritus*, the outline of a man on the cover surrounded by a green halo.

"It's about ghosts in different cultures. Did you know in China they have a whole month where the spirits come up from hell to haunt the living?"

We were sitting on the back porch with Jared, drinking coffee and easing into the day. The slats on the lawn chair dug into my back. Our grass was yellowed and balding, just like the grass in the yards on either side of our chain-link fence. In the backyard to the right, two black poodles snuffled back and forth, their coats matted. The air smelled like diesel and chlorine from the community pool a few blocks down.

"Spring break for ghosts?" I asked.

"The Chinese don't believe in heaven, just different layers of hell," said Jared.

"You guys are making this up."

"My grandmother's Chinese!" said Jared.

"Nobody believes anything anymore," I said.

"You're so cynical, Sarah," Jared said. "I believe in things. I believe in the word of our Lord."

"And I like you despite that," I replied.

Jared sighed. I took a sip of coffee, hot and bitter. I'd asked Rye to pick up milk two days ago, but of course he'd forgotten. 9 a.m. and I was already clammy with sweat.

Rye started to read, "Spirits are like worms or maggots, they feed on dead things. Through death they replicate themselves. But they can be ingested by the living, when they feed on ... uh ... the corpses of animals. Often, they will pass harmlessly through the digestive tract, but they can become embedded in the intestines and from there pass into the blood. Spirits can also become attached to the living, like burrs, when they walk in haunted places. Although invisible due to their small size, they are indeed physical beings, that can usually, but not always, be eradicated through physical means, such as the drinking of vinegar or ...

"Vodka?" I asked. "If so, I should definitely be ghost free."

"Sounds like bullshit," said Jared.

"Or maybe we're all infested with demons," said Rye. "That would explain some things."

He looked toward the sky. "I'm up to my eyeballs in demons," he muttered.

Gray clouds sagged low, shedding a damp fog that did nothing to lessen the day's heat. I couldn't see the refinery, but I could smell the sweet corn stench.

"Maybe ghosts are an STD?" Jared ventured.

Jared was the assistant manager of a Dominos seven blocks down. He came from a religious family, so he'd waited until marriage to have sex and ended up divorced at 20. In the ten years since then, he'd eschewed women and intoxicants, saving up enough money to buy a house. I'd known as soon as I met him that he'd give us the room for dirt. Jared was an odd one, the type who enjoyed both the security of rules and the breaking of them, as long as the breaking was done by someone else. Guess that's what drew him to Rye.

"Why not?" said Rye. "That would make a lot of sense."

He grinned and winked, put his hand on my thigh. His smile could still melt me sometimes, that gap-toothed, don't-blame-me assuredness. But now it was like a knife in my stomach.

"Sometimes a spirit will become infatuated with a member of the living," Rye continued. "It will stalk the love object, hover at the periphery of their life until either the obsession fades or ..."

Something slithered down my spine. I thought of the burning man. I'd been trying to convince myself it was just a dream, but this morning the books I'd knocked over in panic were still fanned haphazardly across the ground. They definitely hadn't been like that when I'd gone to sleep. Maybe I was going crazy. *The call is coming from inside the house.*

Rye's fingertips scuttled up and down my ribcage like spiders' legs. He continued reading.

"Or the spirit will attempt to join with the love object."

"What does *that* mean?" Jared asked.

Rye shrugged and dropped the book onto the stubbled grass.

"The guy's a lunatic."

Bleached light leaked through a gap in the clouds. I moved my lawn chair to the edge of the porch and stuck my legs out. It was Friday, I could make a couple hundred bucks tonight if things went well.

Jared stood up and walked inside. The fog stifled the light.

Rye kneeled next to my chair. He pulled up my shirt, rubbed rough circles on my stomach. Often lately I woke in the night with him on top of me, begging *please, please Sarah.* I could deal if it was sex he wanted, but he needed every inch of me touching him, sweaty flesh threatening to merge. He was dreaming, easy to push away, but it was hard for me to get back to sleep after.

Now Rye's face slid against mine, chin rough with stubble, mouth soft and stale-tasting.

"Mi corazón es una boca," he whispered.

I tried to push him away.

"Stop! I haven't even brushed my teeth!"

Rye stood up.

"You're never home at night anymore. I'm lonely. I know that's pathetic, you need to work … I just … Shit, I start thinking about the knives in the kitchen, if they're sharp enough. Feeling like my blood is drying up in my veins, like I need to see it flowing to know I'm alive."

"Do you want to go back to your dad's house?"

We looked at each other and we were both thinking of the last time we'd slept at Rye's dad's house, locked in the bathroom, curled up together on a bed of towels while his dad screamed drunkenly at no one and kicked at the door. Rye could have easily overpowered him, especially in that state, but he refused to lay a hand on his father, something I'd never understood.

"No," Rye shook his head, "there's nothing there for me anymore."

The sun emerged, white-hot, behind Rye, lighting up his blond hair. He squinted up at the roof, like he was looking for answers there.

I made my hands into a frame, seared the moment into my brain.

Click.

After days of threat, the sky began to rumble. I ran toward the bar, hoping to beat the worst of the rain. Trash skittered across the sidewalk. The air was velvet with damp.

I threw open the door. Sean's gaze ricocheted past me, then back to the television. A rake dragged through me. I hated it when he did this. I wasn't even late. Sean was washing glasses, ignoring his vibrating phone. He was cagey about his home life, but I'd seen the picture of the pretty blonde bouncing in the corner of his screen.

The glasses clinked against the metal basin. Roger coughed. I threw my purse down, grabbed the whiskey and walked over to top him off. There was an odd, chemical scent coming from him. Bug spray. He smelled like he'd bathed in the stuff.

Pawn, Pawn, Pawn blinked red through the mist outside. Cans clattered down the sidewalk. A plastic bag slumped against our glass storefront.

A group of girls wearing damp shirts over bikini tops stumbled into the bar. Probably spent the day drinking down at the river. With them was a dude with scuzzy blond dreadlocks, constellations tattooed across his temples, wearing a studded leather jacket. His name was Heel. He was called Heel because he always carried scavenged bags of bread with him to share, stale pastries he lifted from the dumpster of a local bakery. When none of the girls were looking, he raised his eyebrows at me and doffed an imaginary hat. *So that's how it's going to be.*

Then the sky opened up, rain pummeling the ground so hard that gravel bounced upward. More river rats surged in the door. Girls screamed in delight and boys laughed and licked at the water dripping down their faces. The floor was already filthy. Sean would probably make me mop it before I left, standing and watching me until it was spotless.

Heel threw a couple dozen twenties onto the bar, smirked at me.

"Tequila for everyone!" he screamed.

The crowd cheered. I wanted to ask him what kind of hustle he'd gotten into, but I didn't want to be the one to acknowledge that we knew each other. I remembered his fingers fumbling at my tits, wriggling under my bikini top. *Cmon Sarah, no one will know. Cmon. Please.* On and on until I finally gave in and let him put it in my mouth. The sour taste lingered on my tongue for days.

I lined up a dozen shot glasses and poured. Lightning cracked, and I spilled over the lip of the last glass. *Crap.* Heel took several shots, licked the spilled tequila from the wood. I wanted to grab his filthy hair and slam his face into the bar, claw the stars from his temples. Afterward, I'd been so grossed out that I'd stumbled the mile through the woods to my parents' house. Rye never even noticed that I was gone.

I grabbed my purse, pinched Sean on the back as I passed him and inclined my head toward the bathroom.

A wad of wet toilet paper was stuck to the wall. The concrete was covered with layers and layers of graffiti: poems and pleas, gossip, a cartoon woman with a wolf crawled up inside her, licking the walls of her womb. My stomach cramped. I'd forgotten to eat dinner again. I took the pregnancy test from my purse, ripped open the wrapper.

When I pictured my baby, I imagined one of the tiny fetus dolls our teacher gave us in health class, lodged safely in my guts, perfect and plastic. It glowed with a gentle rosy light; it would never grow or change. The thought of being pregnant didn't fill me with panic, even though I couldn't keep it. Even if I was a fuck-up at least my body could do something right. There was a weird kind of hope in that.

I peed on the white tip and set it on top of the toilet paper dispenser to wait. I'd done this before. The glob of paper on the wall sucked loose and fell to the floor.

Someone knocked. Tipsy girls giggling. I wrapped the pregnancy test in toilet paper, put it in my bag and opened the door. Fighting the urge to snap at them, I hustled back behind the bar.

Onscreen, a black and white movie played, giant spiders that looked like mangy parade floats covered in black fur menaced a blonde-haired woman in a white dress. A blinding light appeared in the middle of the frame. *The fuck?* I'd seen this movie many times before and that wasn't right. The light filled the screen, so bright I had to cover my eyes, then resolved itself into dancing white flames, at their center a motionless blackness in the shape of a man.

The burning man grew larger and larger, until he took up the whole screen. His light-colored eyes met mine, the only part of him I could see clearly. They began to bubble and melt like runny egg-whites. His mouth opened. A black hole, it sucked the fire into it, spinning and spinning.

"You alright doll?" Roger asked. I looked at him, rheumy amber eyes, and when my gaze lurched back to the screen the woman was fighting off one of the spiders with a rake, and the burning man had disappeared. I cleared my throat.

"Fine ... just déjà vu."

"I know what you mean, feels like I've been living the same day over and over ..."

"Yeah?"

"The last thing I remember before this, I was with my wife in the hospital."

"When did she die?"

"13 years ago."

"Do you miss her?"

Roger nodded. "Love's too peaceful a word for what we had ... but now that I have peace. Well, if you want my opinion, it's fuckin' overrated." He raised his whiskey.

"I'll drink to that," I said, fumbling a glass and filling it halfway with Jack. Light speckled my vision, the outline of the man lingering. I gulped a stiff mouthful, then another, burn spreading through me like sluggish lightning. I braced myself against the bar.

It was 12:30. No one had come in for half an hour, since Roger had stumbled home. Sean was out back smoking. He'd be pissed if I followed him, but if I didn't tell him now, I was afraid I never would.

I loved the smell of concrete after the rain, the way the world looked: baptized clean. An odd euphoria took hold of me. Sean sat on a milk crate, the tip of his cigarette lighting up his face. He turned toward me, mouth curved with desire and contempt. I took a deep breath.

"I'm pregnant."

The shriek of the train passing echoed in the alleyway. Sean threw the butt of his cigarette to the ground and crushed it with his boot. He took out his phone and scrolled aimlessly.

"Did you hear me?"

Sean looked at me for a second, rolling his eyes, then back at the phone.

"That sounds like your problem, Sarah."

If I did this, we'd be over. Part of me was looking on, aghast. *There's no we* I reminded myself. *Only you.*

"It's your problem, too, or it will be, if you don't help me."

He scoffed. "How do I know it's mine?"

"I guess you'll just have to take my word for it."

He finally looked up from his phone, the screen reflected in his narrowed eyes. I held his gaze for several seconds, until he cringed and looked away, smashed his hand into the dumpster.

"Motherfuck! I thought you said you were on birth control!"

A hot pressure built behind my eyeballs. I had to play my cards right.

I shrugged. "Sometimes it fails."

His mouth opened and closed, but I couldn't make out what he was saying. All I heard was a piercing static. He spit on the ground next to my shoe. There was a weird satisfaction in seeing his face twisted with emotion, he who was always so controlled.

He took hold of my elbow, dragged me through the door and back inside. Thrust me behind the bar.

"You take care of things here. I'll be back in a few minutes."

He slammed out into the night. My arm throbbed from where he'd grabbed me. I'd never been alone in the bar this late before, under normal circumstances Sean wouldn't have allowed it. Too dangerous.

I wiped down the bar, then drew spirals through the damp with my fingertip, stealing glances at the door. Cloud cover blocked out the moon and stars, the lights of the pawn shop and liquor store long gone dark. Someone could be out there watching me.

Everything felt unreal, my body light, like my organs had been sucked out and replaced with clouds. I traced the panic button beneath the bar. Looking up, I expected to find the burning man staring at me, his fist gripped around the door handle. He would come toward me with his arms raised, and I would finally see his face beneath the veil of flame before he gathered me into his embrace.

Something tickled the back of my neck. The sputter of flames. I whirled around, but nothing was there.

Onscreen the astronaut was tumbling toward the black hole again, the parade of objects orbiting him. If it was a super-massive black hole, you wouldn't be torn apart if you got sucked in, instead time would slow and slow, and you'd be trapped in the fall forever. I pictured myself plunging end over end, fingers grasping at nothing, dragging all the messy debris of my life with me: balls of dirty clothing, Rye and Sean, my parents, their mouths moving mute and angry, empty liquor bottles, a pink lava lamp I'd used as a nightlight until I was in high school, and last of all the burning man, a spinning ball of fire plummeting toward the unreachable center. That must have been what hell was like: stuck forever with your memories and mistakes, your pain, acutely aware but unable to change anything.

I jumped when the door opened. Sean threw a wad of cash down on the bar.

"I want you gone by next week."

His face was flushed, eyes searing gray.

Part of me wanted to go to him, but I grabbed the money and fled, giving him the finger as I slammed the door closed. I wouldn't be coming back. I ran all the way home, not looking behind or around me. If you didn't slow down, if you didn't see the hands reaching for you out of the blackness, they couldn't grab you. It was like being a kid, hiding under the covers while the monster stood over you. As long as you didn't see his face, you were safe.

The porch light was off. I stuck my key in the door and turned on the living room light, took the money from my purse and flattened it on the coffee table. The remnants of incense from Jared's prayer circle still smoldered. 500. Plus the 150 in tips I'd gotten. And the 600 upstairs in the closet I'd been saving for rent. My fingertips tingled. That was enough for a new start, maybe, if your expectations were low and you were carrying nothing but yourself.

I was surprised Sean hadn't asked to see the test, he was usually so meticulous. I pulled it from my purse. Maybe he suspected that I was lying, but he just wanted to get rid of me. It didn't matter what he thought, not anymore. One blue line, the other window empty. Like I was. Cold, black nothingness inside me. Dark matter.

I tiptoed up the stairs. Gathered clothes into a backpack, books and makeup, my computer. On the wall hung a photograph I'd taken down by the river. The water slivered by moonlight, dark shapes floating. Driftwood. When I stared at the picture, the black logs looked as if they were swelling, then shrinking, squirming and flailing. There were infinite other universes with other infinite other versions of me, and some of us stayed and some of us left. I couldn't look at Rye. If I looked at him, I'd be drawn in again, I'd fall down into his body like I always did. The pull of his gravity resisting my escape. I grabbed my broken camera and zipped the bag shut.

I looked around the room to see if I was forgetting anything. I had my passport and license. Downstairs, I grabbed a half-empty bag of chips and a package of mixed nuts. I locked the door behind me. As I walked toward the train station, it started to drizzle again. The lights of the refinery were blurred in the rain and smoke. It looked like a melting city skyline, skyscrapers decaying and on the verge of collapse. A siren echoed through the streets and a chorus of dogs howled in imitation. I opened my mouth and howled along with them.

Within hours I was on a sleek silver train headed out of town, out of the state, my life reduced to the backpack in front of me. We crawled by metal pylons, downtown glowing in the hazy dawn. A train passed slowly in the other direction. Among the passengers, their faces blurred by the rain, the burning man sat calmly in a middle seat, unnoticed by those around him. He didn't look at me. As the train pulled away, a weight slid down my ribcage and disappeared. We passed fallow fields, pastures full of rusted cars. In the distance I saw smoke. Whatever escape I was making, I could one day be pulled back. More troubles would come to me. But for now, my heart was a riot. Silhouettes of mountains loomed in the distance. I gritted my teeth against whatever was to come.

Adriane Hanson grew up by the river in Richmond, VA. She received her MFA in Fiction from Virginia Commonwealth University in 2013. Since then she has lived in mining towns throughout the West, including the highest city in America, (Leadville, Colorado) and Moab, Utah. She has worked as a preschool teacher, editor, bartender, high school English teacher, lifeguard, professor and as an extra on the TV show Westworld. *Her writing has been published in* Monkeybicycle *and nominated for a Pushcart Prize. She now lives in the mountains of Montana where she is raising her son and working on a desert horror novel. She can be found online @instantghosts on Bluesky and Twitter.*

BETWEEN
THE CHANNELS

Steve Toase

Enamel chips and the iron underneath corrodes. The water gets in and rots the metal, unseen and unhalted. And so it is with the projector that rises from the center of my dining table, rust spots showing where the edges got knocked over the years.

Nothing made it out of my granddaughter's house uncorrupted. Certainly not Danielle when they carried her in a transparent white body bag, lifted by two paramedics to keep up appearances of dignity. The projector, the only thing of hers I was able to keep, stood no chance. And the business card tucked in the top. I take it out of my pocket, turning it over and over, reading the name "Mr Aisgill," phone number written between the cloud of mystical symbols, and tuck it away once more.

I reach under the table and check the plumbing connections. Of course, the projector is imperial fittings and in my house everything is metric. I was able to afford to update my house in a way she never could.

All the connectors are wrapped with emergency repair tape. I check again, feeling for any water leaking out of the pipes. Finding none, I make my way to the kitchen, step over the clutter of pans across to the sink and find the stopcock, flinching slightly at the bloom of limescale around the joint. Turning it anti-clockwise, I listen to water gush as the system refills and I wait.

Pressing the on button, I can picture Danielle repeating the same action, her nicotined finger wearing away the faint printed symbols. Somewhere inside the device there is the sound of pressure building. A fine mist that is little more than smoke appears above the Delftware petals. The air smells slightly of chlorine. I press another sequence of buttons, shuddering at a muscle memory that isn't mine. Grease-stained lenses sparkle with light and flicker, then fill the center of the projector with uncertain shapes.

The focus dials are notchy and it takes some patience to settle the image. Some kind of variety show re-run is playing. The figures start vague, then fill out as I watch. A couple tango across the stage, plump limbs shaped in heated water.

I watch the silent jerky movements before turning it off. The projector sighs and the vapor falls from the air to collect in the tiny reservoir. I open the small tap to drain it away, imagining the forced jollity of light entertainment was the last thing she watched. I do not touch the projector for another two days.

The ghosts come soon when I find the dead space between the channels, and splinter the scent blocks into the hollow at the center of the projector. Tuning to them was easy as if the settings were used to this gap between places.

The vapor fills with static, gray snow, and I almost reach out and put my hand in the air to see if it is cold to the touch. I do not, as I've seen scalds before and have no desire to feel the sensation of my own skin sloughing off.

They are faint at first, tasting the familiar in the vapor, and slowly dressing their limbs and torsos in the water. Finally, their heads unfurl from their chests, eyes of phosphorus staring as they shift in the confines of the projector.

I do not recognize them, though I know they have lived in the house for a long time. Silent and lost. Trapped between plaster and brick. Smeared against a house that outlived them all.

Reaching underneath, I unfasten the drainpipe, and hold the end into a plastic pot. Turning off the projector, the ghosts fall as the vapor falls, and I catch the rushing water, tightening the lid before any can escape.

For several days I repeat the process. I do not know if the same ghosts appear, or if new ones manifest each time. They are faint and always uncertain of their own form. A house can hold infinite presences that take up no space, until I give it to them. Each time I unfasten the drainpipe and collect the used water in my small plastic pot. When it is full, I mark it with "1" and start another.

They cremated her, my granddaughter, so she took up even less space in the dirt than she did on the land. They let me take the ashes. There was no money in keeping them as they did everything else.

I spread newspaper on the carpet like she used to when polishing her shoes for the week, and I tip out the powder that was once a person, sorting through for the fragments of bone that even the flames and grinders could not reduce. There is not much to show for twenty-five years on a planet.

The jar of perfume is small and mainly empty. I pour a few drops into the projector's central reservoir and watch the bone fragments float on top. The room fills with the scent of her skin; honeysuckle and witch-hazel. I have to wait a few moments before I can continue.

The projector comes to life, and at first I don't recognize her in the steam, but then it is not the clearest medium to recognize anyone. She is not frail or broken. She is not bent by grief, and when the figure moves around within the snow of the untuned signal they walk with no pain.

She does not recognize me. The eyes that glitter from signal interference cannot see me. For a moment I consider letting the heat blister my skin, just for one more chance to hold her hand, but there is no hand to hold. Not yet. I hold off disconnecting the drainpipe, watching her dance in the vapor. I think she waves, and that is too much for me. I turn off the projector and collect the used water. It smells faintly of honeysuckle.

The knock is confident, as if it is a certainty that the deliverer of the knock should be on the other side of the door. I get up and let the man in. He looks exactly as he does in his photographs. His hair is bleached as are his teeth. He is well-fed and the collar of his pressed linen shirt is slightly too tight against his neck.

"Mrs. Summerscale, I presume," he says, as if he is welcoming me, not the other way around. I nod and shake his hand.

"Mr. Aisgill," I say. "Please come in."

He walks past me and sits down in the only armchair. I turn around one of the dining chairs to face him.

"How did you find out about me?" he says, smiling with each syllable.

"I came across one of your social media adverts," I lie.

He nods, a look of sympathy on his face.

"Many of the bereaved find me that way these days. It's the word of mouth for the new age."

I nod. Even though he is a small man, he takes up a lot of space in the room, and when he leans forward the space shrinks even further in his presence.

"So, how can I help you?" he asks, sympathy dripping from his voice.

I look down at my shoes. He's not the only actor in the room.

"I was watching a comedy the other night," I say, pointing toward the projector. "While changing programs, it got stuck on some untuned gap between the channels."

"It looks like a very old model," he says, peering at the projector. "One of the first generation."

"Second," I correct him. "The first were bare metal, but rusted too quick from the vapor."

He looks at me for a moment, and I wonder if I've blown it.

"It was my sister's," I say to fill the space. "After she went into the nursing home, I did some research to see how much it was worth."

He sits back in the chair and nods.

"I saw some figures in the static, but I wasn't sure," I say.

"It's quite common. The dead seem attracted to the gaps between," he says. "You see the dead don't have any form, and they crave it—"

"Do you think they are ghosts then?" I ask. He settles into his sales patter and the only thing I contribute is to punctuate his monologue with nods.

"The thing with the dead is they crave shape. They have nothing to anchor themselves to in the real world. So, the combination of the untuned signal and the vapor gives them somewhere to place themselves. To become. Now, the problem with that is they still have no voice. No way to communicate with the living. That's where I come in. I can of course talk to the dead when they're non-corporeal," he laughs, and I join in, hoping he does not see this is just a mask.

"But once they take form in the projector it is much easier for someone in my line of work to communicate their needs and desires."

"So, you're a conduit?"

"I fulfill the role of certain senses the dead no longer have. They can see and hear through me. I give them a voice, and that is something that cannot come from water vapor. Of course, my services are not cheap, but I do guarantee results."

"I've read your testimonials."

He holds out his mobile, ready for me to transfer the money across.

"It's half price for the first session, and if you're satisfied then we can discuss a payment plan going forward."

I search my pockets for my own phone, click through to the app and ready the transfer, tapping my device to his and watching the debit go through. I saw the payment plan he agreed with my granddaughter. The credit agreements and the responsibility of the estate. For a moment I think my mask is going to slip, but I maintain my cover.

He smiles and I smile back.

"Would you like a cup of tea," I say, standing, and walking halfway to the kitchen.

"That would be lovely," he says, smiling. Perfect teeth. Perfect bleached teeth.

"I'm afraid I've only got Earl Grey," I say, hand on the kitchen door handle.

"It's all I drink these days," he says. "In the work I do it helps to have delicate flavors."

"I'll be back in a few minutes," I say and close the door.

. . .

I take longer than I need to make the drinks, watching through the gap as he opens cupboards and drawers. Looking for bills to see my financial position. See how long he can drain my accounts for. I pour his tea into the already-prepared cup and avoid inhaling the steam.

He tries to hide it, but I notice him flinch as he takes the first mouthful.

"Sorry. I think the milk is on the turn," I say.

He returns himself to serenity once more. I notice a small patch of grease at the corner of his mouth. He notices me staring and wipes it away, then drains the cup. This is part of the act. The comfort with hospitality. The ability to drink in gifts and offerings like some kind of ancient godling.

He puts the cup on the windowsill, being careful to place a coaster underneath.

"Shall we get started then?"

We take up positions on either side of the projector. I operate the switches, watching the vapor rise between the petals. Once the mist is held in place, I turn on the lenses and tune the device to a midway point between the channels.

The ghosts unfurl, arms and legs spreading across the shifting medium of the mist, like shadows seen in waterfalls. I watch their eyes open, pinpoints of light. His performance starts straight away.

He grasps my hand as if it is a fix, palm damp against mine. His head tips back and his eyes roll away. The full service. The voices come in different registers, shifting and dancing until they settle on a woman who died in her fifties. My aunt Bella

He's good. Every detail I seeded across the internet for him to find is there in his portrayal. The slight West Country accent. A hint of lung damage from the cancer that eventually took her fictional life. The reassurances and platitudes of the professional. Happy place. No more pain. He hits all the beats. I imagine my granddaughter watching the same show, his acting skills giving voice to her husband. The person she trusted more than anyone.

I do not know who the ghost in the mist is. Whether they are one that has appeared before, one I milked of their essence, or someone new. I suspect that the walls are full of fragments of the dead. I've seen them all my life.

• • •

The spirits he's created for his show-and-tell leave him. He slumps back against the chair, exhausted. I make him the second cup of tea. He sips it, preparing himself this time not to flinch at the slight taste of fat. I watch him drink.

"I don't think I've ever had a spirit make themselves known with such presence," he says "With such vigor, but with such frustration that they couldn't say everything they wanted to. Do you feel that you got everything you needed?"

He pauses and puts his hands on his knees to catch his breath as if the effort of acting such a simple role has exhausted him. I do not sympathize. My role is far more complex. Playing the weak and vulnerable when I am anything but. I turn off the projector and the ghosts fade, the last thing to go their eyes as if they are watching him to see what happens next.

"Maybe we should book another session straight away, while I still have space in my schedule. I have lots of regulars, but I feel that I have important work to do here," he says. "Important healing work that you need."

I nod and pick up his cup. He has not questioned why I have not had a drink myself. He is used to getting things others don't. In the kitchen, I run a finger through the thin smear of fat around the rim of his cup.

That was the hardest part to source. Grease from a hanged man. By the time you've reached my age you've been to a lot of funerals and know a lot of undertakers, and there are a lot of suicides out there. I watch him through the open door. He goes to stand and looks nauseous, falling back into his chair.

I do not know how long it takes the dead to shift from the liquid in his stomach to the muscles and nerves of his chest. The marrow of his ribcage. Soon they are in his jaw. In the enamel and pulp of his teeth. He tries to speak and cannot.

I say nothing, as I walk across to the sideboard and unlock the drawer. Take out the photo of Danielle, my beautiful granddaughter. Bereaved twice. Once through the loss of her husband and once through the loss of everything else. I stand the frame in front of him. She recognizes herself and dislocates the unfamiliar bones as she wrests control away from the fraud made authentic.

"I love you, Nan," she says. The words and intonation are hers though the voice is not quite right. I know there are other ghosts spiraling around inside the man in front of me. I do not care about them. I only care about her.

"I can't stay," she says. "This flesh is old and rotten."

"I know," I say, and take her hand. His hand. I can see him trying to fight the spirits inside him, but there are too many. I wonder how he feels to be the genuine article for once in his life. The true channeller of the dead.

"Can you feel me?" I say.

They shake their head.

"Not really," they say. I nod. The fragment of bone is the final piece I have, and the perfume is nearly empty. I pour them into the center of the projector, and turn it on. Heat atomizes the scent. Even though I know Danielle no longer lives, though I am talking to her, I think she has just walked into the room in person instead of squatting in this corrupted meat. The thing that was Mr. Aisgill smiles, but I can tell it's Danielle smiling.

"My favorite," she says. The figure unfurls in the fumes, dressed in the fragrances of honeysuckle and witch hazel. Dances in the mist.

They stand. I can see Mr. Aisgill still fighting, and I admire him for that at least. She walks him across to the projector, and as much as I wish I could see her gait in his steps I cannot.

His neck strains as he realizes what she is about to do, but there were too many ghosts in the water he drank willingly and they are working together.

Steam blisters his chin and lips as he inhales, swelling his tongue, eyelids laminating into thin sheets of peeling skin. I imagine the sensation of burning alcohol condensing deep in his lungs, burning away his voice, his gums fusing to the raw skin of his cheeks. The figure in the projector has gone. When I look at his scorched face, I see a smile I recognize and smile back. The ghosts walk him toward the door, out into the street. Later I find traces of his blistered skin on the door handle.

When I hear the emergency sirens a few minutes later I go out to watch, watch them load him onto a stretcher. I hear later that they saved him, kept alive with pumps and oxygen, and I do not feel a moment of sympathy for the man who bereaved my beautiful granddaughter a second time and me only once but totally.

Steve Toase was born in North Yorkshire, England, and now lives in the Frankenwald, Germany. His fiction has appeared in Analog, Nightmare Magazine, Shadows & Tall Trees 8, Three Lobed Burning Eye, The Deadlands, *and* Shimmer *amongst others. His stories have been selected for Ellen Datlow's* Best Horror of the Year *series, and Paula Guran's* Year's Best Dark Fantasy and Horror. *He also likes bonsai forests, old motorbikes, and vintage cocktails. His debut short story collection* To Drown in Dark Water *is published by Undertow Publications. You can find him at stevetoase.co.uk*

THE BEAUTIFUL THING YOU ONCE WERE

J. Ashley-Smith

Perhaps I should have been surprised when the magpie first spoke. Strange as it may seem, I had become quite used to the mimicries of those curious backyard birds, with their pristine black-and-white feathers, their inquisitive orange-red eyes. Their infamy as deadly swoopers, as springtime terrors of the skies, is legend here in Australia. But I'd never myself been swooped, always associated them rather with their mellifluous warblings, their impersonations. Maybe you remember, too, back when we first moved here as Ten Pound Poms, over half a century ago now, that time a magpie perfectly imitated the mew of our first cat: the irascible ginger, Mr Bentley. Now that *was* a surprise. Hearing his unmistakable complaints and turning to see not a raggedy ball of orange fur padding toward us across the garden, but an impostor, now hopping, now strutting, peering at us from first one eye, then the other. That muggy afternoon, so many summers ago, the magpie held its beak high and let forth another meow, both throatier and more pure than Mr Bentley's, but in all other details precisely correct. Since then, I've heard magpies imitate all kinds of odd sounds: a neighborhood dog; the onomatopoeic calls of currawongs; and once, the rising and falling groans of a leaf-blower. I was so used to their strange calls, I would hardly have paid this one any mind, if it hadn't spoken with your voice. And addressed me by name—the name no one had ever called me but you.

You were inside then. Of course. It had been weeks since I'd tried to wheel you out to catch a ray of sun. I'd given up hope the world of color and light might ever again penetrate the blank windows of your eyes. That day I hadn't even gotten you out of bed, though our nurse—the kindly, patient Miss Little—was always reminding me not to leave you too long in one position; forever doing her bit to keep your bedsores from flaring up again.

I was having one of *those* days. A day where, no matter how sweetly the sun shone or the birds sang, all I felt was despair. Our small suburban home felt like a prison, the walls too close, too cluttered with reminders of how wonderful our life had been. And everywhere, in every room, the smell of you. Not the old familiar smells: the musky odor of your shirt from an afternoon digging the garden, or the tang of your cologne on those rare nights you got all dressed up. The new, alien smells of disinfectant, of human waste, of a body that could perform little more than the most elementary functions. It was one of those days where some bitter and selfish part of me said again and again how this wasn't what I signed up for, that a marriage wasn't supposed to be a death sentence. One of those days where an aged care facility beckoned. Putting you in a home would mean the death of our superannuation, would mean I could eat nothing but potatoes till the end of my days. And you'd made me swear I'd never—not ever—banish you to one of those hideous institutions ... "Put a pillow over my face, Nance. Let me die. I don't want you to remember me as no vegetable." That's what you always said. And yet here we are.

It was hardly past ten, the day looming ahead of me like the shadow of our old elm. I'd taken my cup of tea and a biscuit out into the front garden, out beneath that ancient, elephantine tree, to have an early elevenses and watch the empty quiet of the neighborhood. Cockatoos bickering over seed outside our neighbors' front gate. A bearded gentleman running, with a dog strapped to his waist. A harried mother, with one in the pram and another trailing along behind. I was just beginning to wonder—not for the first time—if I would feel any different caring for you now if we'd ever had children of our own; if there were some maternal instinct that would have switched on, made me more competent, less resentful. But then I heard your voice, clear as day and right beside me.

"Nance," you said. Only it wasn't you, but the magpie, strutting among the leaf litter, grubbing around under the mulch with its beak. "Nance," it said again, and cocked its head, peered up at me with one wary eye.

"Sidney?" I said, and felt immediately absurd.

The magpie said nothing more, though I coaxed it, even broke off a little of my biscuit. The moment it snagged the crumbs in its beak, it beat its wings, took off for a high bough of the eucalypt beyond the power lines. Though it sang from its perch there, throaty and melodious, I felt strangely abandoned. A seventy-year-old woman with a cold cup of tea, alone.

• • •

It was days before I saw the magpie again, though I took my tea and biscuit out to the elm each morning; and each morning, impatient, a little earlier than the last. And though I scattered oats on the kitchen window sill and on the steps outside our front door, it did not return.

The drudgery of care felt oppressive. Those few days stretched endless, a porridge of stagnant time that even the relentless cycle of chores could not budge. I had no patience—with anything, but with you in particular. As I scrubbed you down in bed the way Miss Little had shown me, or dragged you up to heave your dead weight across to the commode, or shoveled into your drooping mouth that morning's colored goop, I was seething, hating you, wanting—forgive me—to hurt you. In my impatience I lost all interest in those quiet pastimes that had kept me sane since your decline: Wordle, the daily crossword, Scrabble on the iPad. All I wanted was to see the magpie, to hear it speak my name, the way you used to when you could say anything at all.

Outside the prison of the house, though, all was beautiful—transcendently so. A late spring after a wet winter, the interminable rains of another La Niña, and the usual dustbowl of our front lawn was thick and verdant.

The camellias along the front of the house were all in bloom, pink and white and red. And the elm, still spindly from the winter months, was just beginning to sprout its first pale bursts of leaf. All about the neighbourhood, acacias frothed with blossom, brilliant yellow fireworks frozen in time. I took my little breaks out in the garden, on the bench seat beneath the elm, where, in earlier, happier times, we two had sat on summer evenings, sipping a G&T, the charcoal smell of the barbecue wafting from the back garden. Now I sat there alone, while inside you rasped your awkward breaths, lips slack, your empty eyes staring at ... what exactly? Did you see anything beyond the blank walls of our old spare bedroom? Did you hear the sounds of spring outside? Did your mind—such as it is now—take you ... anywhere? Did you remember *anything* of us? Of me? It would be so much easier to endure all this if I only knew you were still in there. If I could catch even a glimpse in that living corpse of the man I loved—the man I still love, wherever he is.

Taking my breaks out on that bench beneath the elm, my eyes scanning the trees and bushes round about for a glimpse of the magpie, I became slowly aware of another world existing within our own. A world of signals and warning calls, of wingbeats and ritual displays. The daytime quiet of our suburb, I found, was not so quiet at all, the air alive with the booing of doves, the bickering of cockatoos, the wing snaps of Indian mynahs defending their territory. I'd never noticed before just how many birds there were, all around us, every day. The butcherbirds, the wattlebirds, the families of choughs. The cuckoo shrikes and fantails, and king and superb parrots. I didn't know any of their names at first, but soon dug around in the bookshelf for your old *Slaters Field Guide*, took it out to the bench with my cup of tea. I was so engrossed trying to work out if I'd seen a lorikeet or an eastern rosella, I didn't notice the magpie return, had no sense of its presence until, again, it spoke.

"Nance," it said. "Hullo, Nance. Why the long face?"

So many days had passed since that first encounter that I had begun to doubt myself, was beginning to question whether I'd really heard what I thought I heard. It was like an old cassette tape I played over and over, and with each replay the memory faded, became fuzzier, more indistinct. If you hadn't spoken again—if *it* hadn't spoken—I don't know if I would have continued to believe.

And yet here again was the magpie, hopping around at my feet, pecking at the crumbs of digestive I tossed down, tilting its head to peer at me with one orangey-red eye.

"Hullo, Nance," it said again. "Why so sad, Nance?"

And wasn't it just like you to ask that; such a stupid question. As though there were only ever two ways to feel, and to be anything other than happy was some kind of moral failing. It used to make me so cross whenever you interrogated my moods, said, "Cheer up, Nance." I'd shut myself off from you, simmering away. And with nowhere to go, that feeling would build up inside me like pressure, would turn to anger directed at you, at all the ways you didn't understand me. But that was back when I thought we would go on like we were forever, that we had all the time in the world.

"I'm not sad," I said to the magpie. "I'm ..." My shoulders tensed. "It's complicated."

The magpie moved its beak this way and that, then back again. Strange, jerky movements punctuated by a glance from first one eye, then the other. I realised it was shaking its head.

"Nope," it said. "It i'nt complicated. It's you, Nance, what's complicated. You always was."

My throat began to ache like I'd swallowed a Scrabble piece. But I didn't cry. I was too stunned. Not because I was being psychoanalysed by a magpie—that I had already become oddly accustomed to. But because, maybe, it wasn't a magpie at all, but *you*, speaking through a magpie. To hear again your voice, however scratchy and distorted, to feel again your concern, your warmth, your boundless tolerant love for me, it hurt worse than anything I've ever had to endure; worse because bound up in it was a kind of joy, an ecstatic happiness I'd not felt in years and had forgotten possible. I'd had no time to grieve your loss. You departed by slow degrees, leaving your body behind. And though that reminder was always with me, I'd forgotten *you*, confusing my memory of you with that rasping, dribbling, shitting *thing* in the house. It would have been easier if you'd died.

My eyes were blurry with tears, but you didn't seem to notice, hopping about in the mulch, investigating an empty snail shell, poking at a peg I'd dropped weeks ago. I wiped my eyes and watched you pecking at some unseen treat among the leaves, my heart a leaden thing.

And it's funny, but as the magpie hopped about, doing its magpie business, I began to think how much it reminded me of you. Its restless energy. Its curiosity. I found myself remembering that distant you, the man I first fell for, little more than a boy, and me so stuck up and proper. I remembered Brighton beach in 1972, you in those ludicrous shorts, your legs so skinny, capering about in the sand trying to get a laugh out of me. And you, running down into the water and diving right in, even though it was freezing and filthy. I got all prim over how you shortened my name, acting shocked at how common you were. But it excited me too. *You* excited me. Enough to say yes when you asked me to marry you, to walk with you up the aisle, then up the gangplank of a ship bound for Australia; our permanent honeymoon. I don't know if I ever told you, Sidney. How happy you made me then. How happy you always made me.

"Sidney …" I began. But the magpie had gone.

When at last I went back inside, I found you squirming on the bed, groaning with discomfort. You'd soiled yourself and rolled about in it. All up your back and down your legs was smeared with filth.

The magpie came pretty much every day after that. I'd leave the kitchen window open, crumble walnuts or bits of digestive biscuit on the windowsill, which it snapped up with a cockeyed swipe of its beak.

It wasn't so much a fan of the oatmeal. The little piles I left out in the mornings would be abandoned once it had its fill of sweeter, fattier fare. Each morning, I'd open the window and leave out a little food and in only a few minutes the magpie would be there, standing on the sill while I made my cup of tea and helped myself to a small bowl of muesli—oats being good enough for me. But wasn't that just like you, too? I never could get you to enjoy eating healthy.

After breakfast, I'd start on the chores. But something in me had changed and I wasn't committed to them in the same way I used to be. Some impatience had crept in, and a sense of futility. It all seemed so pointless—all of it. Anything other than sitting out on the bench and talking to my magpie was an impediment. I felt like a teenager in love. All I could think about was the moment I'd be out there again—out there with *you*. The *real* you.

Do you remember, Sidney, what it was like back then? What it felt like to be young and so completely in love? I gave you such a hard time, made you work like a dog for every scrap of my affection. But it was all just a mask, that armor I wore—still wear, I suppose. Underneath I was as soft and susceptive as a fledgling, and burning with excitement, with disbelief. I wanted you with all my heart. Wanted you so desperately to want me. Did I ever take it off for you, I wonder, that mask? Did I ever let down my guard enough for you to see how I truly felt, how much you always meant to me?

My elevenses with the magpie were just like those old days, sort of. You, trying everything to make me laugh, cheering me up with silly presents or prancing around in the hope it would make me smile. As I sat on the bench in the morning sunlight, the magpie did his funny little dance, bringing me gifts, a shiny sweet wrapper or a puff of acacia blossom. He'd preen and strut and tell me funny stories. I was happy like I hadn't been in months; years, even. It was as though we'd been given a second chance, you and me, a once-in-a-lifetime opportunity to do it all over again. I vowed to myself that this time I'd hold nothing back, would hide nothing from you.

But I was curious, too. How was it possible? How were you *in* there, looking up at me from those inquiring orange-red eyes, speaking to me from that pointy gray beak? Where were you really? Were *you* the magpie? Or was the magpie just a ... mouthpiece, like a telephone you could call me from whenever you wanted a chinwag? Though I'd grown used to this new and unusual way of being together, some sensible, critical part of me kept nagging, wanted to peer under the curtain, to learn how it was *done*.

"Don't ask that, Nance," the magpie said, whenever my curiosity got the better of me. "Don't ask." And then it would launch into some fantastic story, an anecdote of you and me with all the trimmings, those embellishments you'd always add, as though the day-to-day events of our married life were as packed with drama and romance as any opera. "D'you remember, Nance? D'you remember that time we was …"

And off you'd go.

It was in the middle of just such a story that a car I didn't recognise pulled onto the drive. The magpie squawked and beat its wings; a flash of black and white and it was up in the tree. It was a large, new navy-blue car, big and serious-looking. The driver stepped out, a woman I'd never seen before—as big and serious as the car—with a gray crew cut and a square chin.

"Mrs. Norris?" she said, her voice officious and booming. "I'm Miss Rankin, from the agency. I'm here to replace Miss Little. We called, but you haven't been answering your phone."

It was the nurse—another one. Back already. A week had passed in a moment and I'd hardly noticed. I followed her up the steps to the front door, meekly, though it was my own home and she the stranger. My face was hot and flushed, felt red as the camellias blooming either side of the steps. It was as though I'd been caught in some indiscretion, found by my mother with a boy in my bedroom. I turned on the threshold, glanced back toward the trees hoping to catch a glimpse of my magpie. But you were nowhere to be seen.

A look of outraged disdain puckered Miss Rankin's face. She pressed ahead of me, uninvited, into the house.

"In here?" she said, pushing open the door to the spare room. "Oh, Mrs Norris!"

Lord knows what you'd done, but that body of yours was on the floor, crumpled against the skirting board. One foot was still up on the bed. Your pajamas were soaked with wee and half off, exposing on your legs and back the raw, raging bed sores.

It was terrible, the dressing down that odious woman gave me. She made all kinds of threats, said she'd report me for this and that: maltreatment, malnourishment, neglect. She said I'd been starving you to death. Worse.

I wanted to tell her it wasn't like that, to explain. But how could I tell her the truth? And what even was the truth? That it wasn't you in that room any more than a house is the family who makes their home in it—that the important part of you, the Sidney I held so dear, was with me in the form of a magpie. That we were happier than we'd ever been. Standing shamefaced in the spare room while that wicked nurse raked me over the coals, it all seemed so ludicrous. And you, your shell, so helpless and damaged. I've never felt so guilty, or so foolish.

For more than a week after she'd gone, until days after her next visit, I clung to my chores like a woman drowning. I kept you fed and clean, turned you and tended to your sores, even wheeled you out into the lounge to feel the sun while I did the crossword. I talked to you like I used to, calling out the clues, how many letters they were, which letters we had. But you never said anything—of course you didn't. I didn't go outside to the bench, though the weather was glorious, the chorus of the many birds an open invitation. I told myself I didn't want to, that my place was inside, my duty was to you—to that body of yours. The judgment of the terrible Miss Rankin was like a sack cloth covering my shame, her words a flail with which I whipped myself into obedience. Though I still left food for the magpie, it was only oatmeal, and I left the kitchen window closed.

I saw the magpie only twice in all that time, through the glass of the front door, pacing on the steps. It called out to me, throating its mournful, flute-like warble. The second time, it tapped on the glass with its beak. And though it pained me worse even than the guilt I felt, I didn't go to it. I didn't open the door. The magpie's eyes, as it peered at me through the glass, first with one and then the other, seemed filled with sadness. I turned my back, went into the lounge and closed the door behind me, tried to ignore the tap-tap-tapping from the corridor, tried not to see you slumped in the wheelchair, tongue poking dumbly from your mouth, your chin slick with drool.

The last time the magpie came knocking at my door, I was in the kitchen fixing your food. I heard the tap tap tap of its beak on the glass. It sang a few bars of its morning song—*woodle-ardle-oodle-wardle*—summoning me as surely as if it had pushed the doorbell.

"Go away," I yelled down the corridor. "Can't you see I'm busy?"

"Nance," it said and tapped again. "Come on, Nance, open the door. Let me in, Nance. Let me in."

It was your voice, your words. How could I refuse?

I opened the door and in hopped the magpie. Its claws tapped scratchily on the floorboards as it followed me back into the kitchen. With a beat of its wings it rose to the bench top, peered into the bowl, squawked—the perfect imitation of a cockatoo.

"Yuck," it said. "What's that muck, Nance? Got any biscuits?"

"It's good for you," I said. "Pumpkin, broccoli, chicken. It's all you can eat now. Well, not *you*. You know what I mean."

"Yuck," it said again. "I'd rather be dead than eat that slop. Get the biscuits, Nance."

I crumbled a digestive onto the benchtop and the magpie pecked at it thoughtfully. It cocked its head, peering past me at something. Then it hopped down from the bench and into the lounge.

When I caught up with it, the magpie was pacing the Turkish rug, cocking upward glances at the figure drooped in the wheelchair.

"Bloody hell," it said. "Is that ... Is that what I look like?"

It circled the wheelchair with a series of hops, fluttered up to land on your knee, onto the tartan blanket I'd stretched out there. It peered up at your sagging face, turning its head to peer with first one eye, then the other. It shook its head, hopped up your arm to your shoulder, examined your profile with great care and curiosity. Then, as though in disgust, the magpie shat down the front of your pajama top.

"Gormless sod, in't I?" It said and turned to me. "Put it away, Nance. I can't bear to look at it no more. Put it back in its box."

The magpie flew from your shoulder to mine, perched by my ear like the parrot from *Treasure Island*. I suppose that was the moment I stopped thinking of you, the body, as *you* anymore. I wheeled it back to the spare bedroom, with you gripping my shoulder, chatting away, cheerful as ever.

"That's right, Nance. Just stick it on the bed. Now close the door. That's right. I don't want to see it no more and you shouldn't have to neither. What d'you want with that manky old thing when you've got me for company. Come on, Nance, that's right. Let's go back to the kitchen. You fix yourself a nice cuppa and I'll polish off that digestive. Then you sit down and tell me all about it. It's been too long, Nance. I've missed you."

We slept together that night, for the first time since you went downhill. I lay curled on the bed, and you slept standing on the bedside table. It didn't look at all comfy, but you told me it was fine, that you always slept that way these days and were all the better for it.

I woke in the night to the sound of banging from the next room. Thumping, and a kind of muffled groan. I made to get up and see to it, the needs of the body in the other room, but your voice in the darkness made me pause.

"Leave it, Nance," you croaked. "Leave it. There's nothing in there we need worry about."

I lay back down and pulled up the sheet, closed my eyes.

"That's right. You just go back to sleep. Sweet dreams, Nance."

But I couldn't sleep. I lay there in the dark, as wide awake as if I'd drunk an espresso, listening to the sounds from beyond the wall. The bumps and rattles. The dreadful glottal moans.

When at last I did drift off, I dreamt of flight—soaring, liberating flight.

Those last days were perhaps the happiest of our marriage. Certainly, they were the least complicated.

You knew, I think, how it would end. That, as separate as you were from the body you'd left behind, you were tied to it nonetheless. Bound. Maybe we both knew. And that knowledge lent an electric sparkle to each moment of our last hours together. For the first time in my life, I held nothing back. Not a thing. I felt so free in your company, no longer constrained by my past inhibitions, my innate reserve. I saw you, at last, for who you truly are. For the kind and beautiful soul you'd always been—and always will be, wherever you are now.

We were out on the bench when it happened, in the shadow of our resplendent elm, its leaves now lush and green and whispering gently in the faint spring breeze. You were pecking about in the mulch; listless, you seemed, almost bored. I was drowsy, lulled by the serenity of that blissful morning, the stillness inviolate. The empty street, aglow with sunshine. And the smell of springtime everywhere, the air thick with that heavy fragrance of life, of its endless evanescent flowering. Out of the corner of my eye, I saw you stop, cock your head to the left as though listening.

"Nance," you said. "Listen, Nance. I've got to tell you something."

You cocked your head again, to the right this time. Then froze. You shook out your feathers, like you might to clear them of rain.

"What?" I said. "Tell me what, Sidney?"

But you never replied. The magpie lifted its head, opened its throat and let out a long exultant peal, a warbling, ululant song filled with joy and sadness. And I knew you'd left me.

The magpie took flight. Not over to the eucalypt by the power lines, as usual. But away beyond the rooftops, toward the reserve at the edge of the suburb. I stood, straightened my skirt and went back up to the house.

Your eyes were wide open, your mouth, too. I shut them gently, went into the bathroom for a flannel and the soap. I stripped the bed, peeled off your pajamas, had to loosen them with warm water where you'd soiled yourself and it had dried to a crust. I cleaned you. Not the way the nurse had shown me, but gently, lovingly. Remembering every corner of your old body for what it was: a piece of you, my dear, dear husband.

From the very back of the cupboard I pulled out your wedding suit, unzipped it from the cover. I'd not seen it in decades. There was a dead flower in the lapel, a camellia. The petals crumbled when I touched them. The suit smelled of you, though you'd not worn it in forty years or more. It was too small, of course, so I got out your summer suit instead, the cream one I always liked that made you look so dapper and handsome; the one you always used to wear with that straw hat. I couldn't find the hat, and wouldn't have been able to put it on you anyway, with you all laid out like that. But I dressed you in the suit and a nice white shirt, smoothed the lapels. I lay down beside you with my arm across your chest.

There's a car pulling into the drive. The nurse, I expect. At least I won't be seeing any more of *her*.

Oh Sidney, what am I going to do without you? I don't know if I'm ready to say goodbye.

Perhaps a cup of tea and a biscuit. And then I'll be ready.

J. Ashley Smith is a British–Australian author of dark fiction and co-host of the Let The Cat In *podcast. His first book,* The Attic Tragedy, *won the Shirley Jackson Award. Other stories have won the Ditmar, Australian Shadows and Aurealis awards. He lives with his wife and two sons beneath an ominous mountain in the suburbs of North Canberra, gathering moth dust, tormented by the desolation of telegraph wires. His short story collection,* The Measure of Sorrow, *is out now from Meerkat Press.*

COVER ART

TODAY AND TOMORROW

--- ■ ---

Jing Zhiyong

Jing Zhiyong is a painter living and working in Beijing, China. He graduated from the Oil Painting Department of Tianjin Academy of Fine Arts in 2005 and paints dreams, hopes, and the absurd world.

THANK YOU!

PATREON SUPPORTERS:

Jer Blane

Daniel Gardner, HfB

Todd Gill

Elad Haber

Brent Jones

Anthony Notarfrancesco

Damon Savage

Peter T. Secker

Dave Sturgeon

Tony